CHARLENE
SANDS

THE
CORPORATE
RAIDER'S
REVENGE

Silhouette ®

Desire

Published by Silhouette Books
America's Publisher of Contemporary Romance

SILHOUETTE BOOKS

ISBN-13: 978-0-373-76848-6
ISBN-10:   0-373-76848-6

THE CORPORATE RAIDER'S REVENGE

Copyright © 2008 by Charlene Swink

Visit Silhouette Books at www.eHarlequin.com

Printed in U.S.A.

Recent books by Charlene Sands

Silhouette Desire

Like Lightning #1668
Heiress Beware #1729
Bunking Down with the Boss #1746
Fortune's Vengeful Groom #1783
Between the CEO's Sheets #1805
The Corporate Raider's Revenge #1848

CHARLENE SANDS

resides in Southern California with her husband, high school sweetheart and best friend, Don. Proudly, they boast that their children, Jason and Nikki, have earned their college degrees. The empty nesters now have two cats that have taken over the house. Charlene's love of the American West, both present and past, stems from storytelling days with her imaginative father, sparking a passion for a good story and her desire to write romance. When not writing, she enjoys sunny California days, Pacific beaches, and sitting down with a good book.

Charlene invites you to visit her Web site at www.charlenesands.com to enter her contests, stop by for a chat, read her blog and see what's new! "Friend" her at www.myspace.com/charlene sands or e-mail her at charlenesands@hotmail.com.

This one is for Mom and Dad.
You are always with me.

One

Elena Royal sipped on her second glass of Sex on the Beach and the irony struck her anew.

Sex on the beach?

That's exactly what she should be having right now, while on her honeymoon. Instead, she sat outside alone on a bar stool of the Wind Breeze Resort. As overhead palm frond fans lapped around stealing traces of tropical Hawaiian heat, she cast off admiring looks from men at the patio bar and proceeded to drink away her sorrows.

She would have been married by now.

To Justin Overton, the scoundrel who had her convinced he loved her and not the Royal bankroll. Finding out on her wedding day that her would-be bridegroom hadn't an honest bone in his body, sent her packing,

abandoning her wedding and the guests that would have arrived within the hour.

Yes, she'd left Justin at the altar, but she'd left her heart there, as well. No longer the trusting twenty-six-year-old girl who believed in happily ever after, Elena's tender ego had taken a nosedive.

She'd been shattered and still felt slivers of regret and heartache deep inside. She'd come to this secluded out-of-the-way Maui resort hoping she wouldn't be recognized as the daughter of West Coast hotel magnate, Nolan Royal. She needed the escape. She needed peace and quiet. She needed time to reevaluate her life. She'd spent the past three weeks on the beach, swimming, reading and relaxing.

It was driving her crazy.

The midnight moon glistened on the oversize pool and beyond that, Hawaiian waters caressed the sand, the gentle waves echoing into a soft roar. From under the thatched roof of the bar's hut, she finished her drink, debating on having another before returning to the solitude of her lonely cottage. The sultry June night surrounded her in stillness, the Wind Breeze Resort falling short of its namesake. If it weren't for the lapping fans, the heavy air would smother her.

"Want another drink?" the bartender asked, then darted a hard quick stare, keeping the last of the men at the bar from approaching her.

She smiled. Joe, the bartender, had taken it upon himself to protect her solitude once he realized she

wasn't like other single women who were eager and willing to leave the bar with a stranger. "I'd better not. I haven't finished this one yet."

A splash from the pool had her lifting her eyes from her cocktail glass.

The late-night swimmer dipped down deep in a perfect dive then, shadowed by moonlight, he rose up until his head popped out of the water. Water flowed off longish black silken hair and his shoulders rivaled the breadth of an Olympic athlete.

She caught herself staring and when he spotted her, he stared back, his eyes dark and piercing. Her heart beat faster. Chills of awareness romped up and down her body, the sensation like nothing she'd ever experienced before.

She lifted her lips in a smile.

He didn't smile back, but the slightest arch of one brow answered her.

She grew warm all over, her lower body stirring with unexpected heat as she watched the stunning man come out of the water with a grace that belied his rugged physical stature.

Holding her breath, she watched as he mopped up beads of water off his shoulder, shaking out his hair and wrapping a towel around his waist. He glanced at her again, his eyes filled with promise. Her heart raced as she hoped for his approach, which surprised her since she'd sworn off men at least for the next ten years.

She'd had it with liars, deceivers, men who'd speak vows of love and forever after, only to want a piece of

the Royal pie. Justin had been most clever. She'd been fooled quite easily with his charm and vows of undying love. Until her father had him investigated.

She'd found out just in the nick of time that Justin Overton wasn't the high-powered financial consultant he'd claimed to be when she'd met him in Europe six months ago, but a college dropout on the verge of bankruptcy.

Elena had run for all she was worth to hide away in this tropical resort and heal her broken heart.

She glanced once more toward the pool. Her mystery man was gone. Just like that, he'd disappeared. Elena sighed and shook her head. It was probably for the best. At least her instant attraction meant she wasn't completely destroyed inside, burned somewhat but not yet a dry pile of ashes.

"Anything wrong, miss?" Joe asked, wiping a shot glass clean and keeping his eyes trained on her.

"Nothing at all, Joe," she said, with a quick rueful smile, realizing the only *sex on the beach* she would have tonight remained sitting at the bottom of her sparkling cocktail glass on the bamboo-framed bar.

The combination of peach schnapps, vodka and fruit juices she'd had in those two drinks last night, wreaked havoc on her head this morning. She'd never been a heavy drinker, preferring a glass of vintage wine or fine champagne. Now, she paid the price with a hangover that pounded like a sledgehammer.

She sat on a private stretch of beach on a striped

sand chair, sipping straight black coffee, watching the ocean through her gold-framed sunglasses. Even Yves Saint Laurent couldn't block the bright sunshine well enough to keep her eyes from squinting and her head from aching.

She closed her eyes and hoped the fresh sea breezes would clear out the fuzziness.

"Mind if I take up this piece of real estate?" A deep male voice surprised her eyes open and another chair slid into the sand next to her.

She looked up and found her mystery man smiling at her, his eyes hidden behind a dark pair of Ray-Ban sunglasses. He wore an unbuttoned tropical shirt in blacks and forest greens and dark shorts. The shirt flapped in the breeze, opening enough for her to see that same muscled physique that had inspired her interest last night. "This beach is one big open house," she said, sipping her coffee.

He sat and stretched out his tanned legs. "There's definitely something to be said for the view."

She nodded, looking out at the horizon, until she realized he might have been offering a compliment. She turned to him, but he masked his expression well. She felt his eyes on her through the gunmetal shade of his sunglasses.

"Thanks for loaning me a piece of your private strip of beach. I'm Ty," he said.

"El—uh…Laney," she offered, glad not to be sharing last names and making an attempt not to give her true

first name, either. Only her father and best friend called her by her childhood nickname, Laney. She sipped her coffee again.

"Too much Sex on the Beach last night, Laney?"

Her body flashed hot from the way he said *sex*. He was about as appealing as one man could get and his rich confident voice didn't hurt his image, either.

"Uh, yes to drinking too much and none of your business, if that question went somewhere else."

"It didn't," he said quickly. "I saw you last night at the bar."

"I'm not really much of a drinker."

He smiled and his mysterious persona vanished for a second. "Are you bored?"

"Last night I was," she answered honestly. "I mean, I came here to relax, do some reading, do nothing at all." *Recover from a broken engagement.*

"But doing nothing isn't your style?"

She shook her head. "Apparently not."

He sank back into his chair and watched the waves hit the shore. "It's not my style, either. I guess we have that in common."

"Are you on vacation?" she asked, wondering if he was alone on the island. Not that it should matter one way or the other. She told herself she was simply making idle conversation.

"Something like that," he said with a shrug. "With a little business mixed in. I always stay at the Wind Breeze when I'm here."

* * *

When she leaned back in her chair, Evan Tyler looked his fill. Damn, she was a beauty. Just thinking about the way her smoky blue eyes had nearly devoured him last night made his blood heat. He'd come out of the pool to find this gorgeous blonde studying him from her bar stool with a look of pure lust in her eyes. What turned him on even more was that she was probably clueless as to how she appeared—her body language enough to bring a man to his knees.

Then Evan realized who she was.

Elena Royal.

He'd recognized her from a few photos he'd seen. And though the rich heiress hadn't been notorious, she'd had a broken engagement that made the rounds with every sleazy tabloid in the country.

His rival in the hotel business, Nolan Royal, had only the one child and she usually kept a low profile. He guessed she'd come here to recover from the scandal of leaving her fiancé at the altar. Hollywood had been buzzing with news of the Royal breakup, but Nolan killed the media attention instantly with hefty bribes to unprincipled journalists to let that story die a quick death.

Money talked and people listened. And Evan almost could give Nolan Royal credit for keeping the media out of his daughter's life.

Almost.

But because Nolan Royal had been a *royal* pain in his ass lately, cheating him out of a hotel buyout that

he'd been working on for two years, he couldn't even give the man his due for protecting his daughter. Evan still burned from Royal's deliberate and dishonorable tactics. He'd lost two years of his life and a sizable chunk of future income to Nolan Royal. Yet, the older man had covered his tracks well and Evan couldn't provide any tangible proof that Royal had resorted to shady, if not illegal means to take over the southern-based hotel chain, The Swan's Inns.

Now, Evan was out for blood.

He meant to make Royal pay.

Evan turned to her, noting her bright red two-piece swimsuit that couldn't begin to hide her full breasts and luscious curves. "Want to get *un*bored?"

She raised her eyebrows and he could tell she was intrigued. "What do you have in mind?"

He rose and stripped to his swim trunks then grabbed her hand. "Let's go for a swim."

Laney enjoyed the swim with Ty so much that when he asked her to join him for lunch she couldn't find a reason to veto the invitation. They dined at Moose McGillycuddy's, a local Maui establishment on Front Street in Lahaina. They were known for their Ono Pu-pus, nose-clearing, mouth-searing hot chicken wings.

The place was jam-packed but somehow Ty orchestrated a corner table on the lanai that overlooked the historic town below hopping with tourists. Normally, Laney abhorred crowds and avoided places that

crammed folks in worse than a Stones concert, but Ty promised *nothing boring*. And nothing boring, was exactly what she'd gotten. Studying photojournalism abroad, Laney loved people-watching. They made the best subjects for the camera and she'd been taking pictures of people and events ever since her father pre-sented her with her first Canon on her twelfth birthday, fourteen years ago.

When she wanted to order a simple chicken salad, Ty intervened and made her try something a bit more daring on the menu. She ordered the Kahuna, a burger loaded with teriyaki sauce and grilled pineapple and told him after sharing those hot wings appetizers to be satisfied, because that was as bold as she was willing to go, right now. As she nibbled on her burger, she watched him eat Kalua Pig, a shredded pork sandwich piled high with cabbage and sautéed onions, another of the local main fares.

They walked along Front Street after lunch and spoke of nothing important. She liked that they'd seemed to have a silent agreement, no last names and no personal histories to mar the time they spent together.

She found him exciting and fun and full of surprises. When he took her back to the Wind Breeze, he walked her into the lobby and spoke in a sexy low voice near her ear. "I'd like to explore your 'bold as you're willing to go' comment a little more. Have dinner with me tonight."

She wasn't here for romance. She'd come to this secluded resort to get away from the press and memories that would have surely haunted her much more had she

stayed in Los Angeles after the wedding fiasco. Normally, she wasn't one to sit still, but a broken heart had a way of sucking the joy out of everything. She was here to recover from her emotional injuries, she reminded herself, yet she could use a diversion.

A handsome, attentive diversion.

"Will I be expected to have more Ono Pupus?" she asked with a little smile. "Because my mouth is still burning up from lunch."

His attention riveted to her lips. "I can promise you no more hot wings, Laney." Then he added in a thrilling whisper, "But I'm afraid I can't make any promises regarding your mouth."

A shot of heat rivaling the Ono Pupus coursed through her body and she decided that Ty was good for her torn-up ego. Why shouldn't she have dinner with a fascinating man? Why not have *more* than dinner with him? She'd played by the rules all of her life and look what that got her?

She'd been persuaded by her well-meaning father to enter into The Royal hotel business after college, when all she really wanted in life was to become a photojournalist. And when her father had given her a three-month reprieve to study and tour Europe with her camera, hoping she'd get the camera bug out of her system, she'd met a vacationing Justin Overton in a little French café.

Justin had been smooth and charismatic and she'd been so naive. She'd found that he'd deliberately sought her out, following her from her native California home,

playing on her love of photo galleries and the stunning French countryside. They had so much in common, it seemed, and before long, she fell in love and they'd gotten engaged quickly.

Laney thought she knew Justin well, until her father went against her wishes and had him investigated. And just before they were to speak their vows, her fiancé had been exposed as a fraud and a con man, only interested in Royal money.

He'd duped her, broken her heart and made her look like a fool. That wouldn't happen again with any man, much less an appealing stranger she met today on the beach. Thanks to Justin, she had trust issues now. She would guard her heart well.

So why not have a little fun? Let go and enjoy the rest of her time here, instead of trying to wrap herself around a *New York Times* bestseller thriller. Or pretend to enjoy the sand and surf, when her disillusionment weighed her down like an iron anchor.

"If you're married or engaged, I'll personally hunt you down and have your head on a platter," she said, only half-jokingly.

Ty's laughter filled the lobby and an appreciative gleam entered his eyes. "That's not in the cards for me. I'm single. I can make you that promise."

"Okay then," she said, "I'll have dinner with you."

He glanced at his watch, then cast her a steamy look filled with other promises. "I'll pick you up at eight. Be ready to have some fun and be *bold*."

He left her standing there, untouched. By the hungry look in his eyes, though, Laney knew that might all change tonight and she debated—for about two seconds—whether or not she should have dinner with him after all.

"Find out everything you can about Elena Royal, Brock. I need this info yesterday." Evan spoke to his brother on his cell phone as he drove along the Maui coastline toward the run-down but potentially profitable Hotel Paradise on the western tip of the island.

"Elena Royal?" Brock questioned quickly. "From what I understand, she's made herself as invisible as a person who bears the Royal name could. Except for her recent marriage collision, she's kept herself out of the limelight. What could you possibly want to dish up about her?"

"She's here on the island. We've met and she doesn't know who I am."

"So?"

"So? She's Nolan Royal's only child, only daughter. She's worked for him on and off the past few years."

"She's quite a looker, Ev. I've seen her picture somewhere. Where are you going with this?"

"She's bound to have knowledge of the old man's business. If that hotel chain is truly in trouble, I need to know. I'll make it my mission to find out while I'm here."

"I'll find out what I can right away. How is it, I'm up to my ears in paperwork and you're sunning yourself at an island resort with a gorgeous woman?"

Evan pulled the rented Porsche into the drive leading to the ramshackle hotel and parked the car. He made an instant assessment. Good location. Great view. In need of major renovations. He'd have to do a thorough appraisal before deciding to add this hotel to the Tempest chain, the Tylers' hard-won hotel corporation.

"Someone's got to do it, Brock," he said, amused at the image of his youngest brother sitting behind a desk, knee-deep in work. Brock wasn't one to sit still very long. "I'm one who doesn't mind mixing business and pleasure. They're one and the same for me."

"You know, rumors about the Royals have been floating around for months."

"Precisely. I plan to find out if there's any truth to them. Call me when you have details."

Evan clicked off the phone and got out of the convertible, leaving the car right in front of the porte cochere. No valet. He made a mental note before entering the establishment to tour the hotel with the owner.

By seven forty-five that evening, Evan had showered in his cottage suite at the Wind Breeze, dressed in a black suit and had gotten all the details he needed about Elena Royal. He had to admit, the woman hadn't been dealt a fair hand. She'd been courted by a con man and he'd almost succeeded in landing a place in the Royal family. Nolan had been cagey and going against his daughter's wishes and risking their relationship, he'd had the guy investigated completely, almost too late.

That only showed the hotel baron was getting soft in his old age.

Evan straightened his gray silk tie, combed his hair and grabbed several condoms from an unopened box in the dresser, sliding them into his pocket with ease. He hadn't met a woman who'd intrigued him more than Elena Royal in months and he didn't plan on letting her get away. There was keen intelligence in her eyes. She had a quick wit and an uncanny sense of humor. He'd make sure the lady didn't know another moment of boredom.

At precisely eight o'clock, Evan knocked on her cottage suite and was nearly *knocked* to his knees when she opened the door.

She went for bold.

"Wow." His low appreciative whistle made her smile almost shyly.

"Thank you," she said, bowing gracefully, her long wavy blond hair falling over her shoulders. Sleek black lacy material dipped low and Evan eyed her awe-inspiring cleavage and the way the dress hugged her body at the waist, curving around perfect hips to rest just above the knees. She appeared taller, almost eye level with him now, thanks to shiny rhinestone-embellished sandals that lifted her up about four inches.

"Come in for a second. I need to get my purse." When she turned around, soft folds of that lacy material plunged down to the very last vestiges of what would be considered decent, exposing her full back, teasing at her shapely bottom and making him itch to uncover more.

He stepped inside the suite's living room and kept his eyes trained on her. "Nice."

"It's almost like home," she said, picking up a small black evening bag from the sofa and turning. "I've been here almost a month."

"In that dress, you have to know I wasn't speaking about the room."

"Oh." She appeared flustered. "Thanks again."

Evan would love to keep her that way all night, with a rosy hue on her cheeks and a glint of anticipation in her eyes. He approached her slowly. "Let's just get this over with."

"Get what over with?"

She seemed genuinely surprised, but Evan couldn't stop himself. "This," he said, wrapping his arms around her, dipping his head and taking her in a hungry kiss. Her lips tasted fruity sweet like tropical nectar from the island and her body felt damn good pressed to his. Her little breathless moan of surprise triggered his desire even more. He deepened the kiss, slanting his head and brushing his lips over hers again with more demand this time. And she responded by putting her arms around his neck and pressing her mouth harder to his.

He parted her lips and stroked her tongue once, twice and she met his strokes with tentative ones of her own. His manhood rose to the occasion and he couldn't figure out if she were an expert tease or more timid than she let on. But he couldn't deny that she felt perfect in his arms. Evan pulled back slightly and looked into her

killer blue eyes. "If I didn't promise you dinner, we wouldn't be leaving this room, Laney."

She shook loose her blond waves and spoke in a breathless whisper, "Well, then I guess it's a good thing you did promise dinner. I like a man who keeps his promises."

"I also promised that you wouldn't be bored."

She released her breath slowly and unwound her arms from his neck. "So far, I'd say you've succeeded. You continue to surprise me, Ty."

Ty? For a minute, Evan almost forgot the real reason he pursued the wealthy heartbroken heiress. Without revealing his identity, he planned on getting some first-hand knowledge about The Royal hotels and any trouble they'd been having lately.

He brushed his mouth to hers again, then grabbed her hand and led her out of the suite, before they wound up horizontal on the bed.

Laney surprised him, too, and that was a tall order. Evan never liked surprises of any kind. He always needed to be in control. His immediate intense reaction to Laney Royal wasn't just sexual and that bothered him. But he wouldn't let that get in the way of what he really needed from her.

Information.

Two

Laney's lips burned now, not from Ono Pupus but from the man named Ty, whose spontaneous kisses had put a whole new meaning to the word *bold*.

Warm Hawaiian breezes blew her hair into a wild new style as they drove in Ty's sports car along the coastline. Laney thought of the lesson her father had always drilled into her head.

Be careful what you wish for.

She'd been lonely and glum without really knowing it, trying to convince herself she was doing fine after Justin's betrayal, but she'd been praying for something or someone to bring her out of her doldrums.

And out of the blue, this striking mystery man had entered her life and suddenly, Elena's heart raced

again. Her body throbbed with excitement. Her nerves tingled and she felt truly alive. She'd gotten what she wished for and now she wouldn't tempt fate by questioning it. She'd decided the moment Ty's lips had touched hers, that she wouldn't deny herself this opportunity to forget the past.

She'd be leaving the island in two days to go home and spend some time with her father. Being the sole heir to the Royal empire, her father wanted her not only to learn the business, he wanted her to *love* the business as much as he did. But Laney never had and she'd always felt like a disappointment in that. She'd tried, but she couldn't become even remotely passionate about his business. Not when her camera was close at hand and there were countless images just waiting to be photographed.

She put all that aside for now. She'd live in the moment with a man who seemed to know exactly where those moments would take them.

Ty took her to an intimate restaurant overlooking the Pacific. They dined on the rooftop where tiki torches and a sliver of moonlight were the only source of illumination. The night was sultry and warm and the sound of waves crashing against the shore rivaled her pounding heart. She had Ty's undivided attention while they feasted on platters of seafood and drank champagne.

After dinner, the select few private rooftop guests were treated to a luau performance with beating drums and Hawaiian dancers whose exotic moves and undulations put Laney in a daring mood. She sipped her

drink and each time she glanced at Ty, she found him watching her with a raw gleam in his eyes.

When the show ended, a three-piece band took over and played mellow tunes. Ty stood and took her hand. "Dance with me."

Laney rose and followed him onto the dance floor. She loved the strength of his grasp, the way she didn't have to think about a thing when she was with him. And when he took her into his arms, meshing their bodies almost too close for her equilibrium, Laney allowed it. She fell into him, resting her head on his shoulder, her body pulsing inside and fully aware of his own growing need.

"I couldn't wait to hold you in my arms again," he whispered into her ear.

"I couldn't wait, either," she whispered back.

He brushed a soft kiss to her throat, then another and worked his way up to her chin, while his hands wreaked havoc on her back, his fingers splaying along the top of her derriere.

They rocked back and forth, more in rhythm to their own bodies than to the music playing.

"How long are you on the island?" he asked quietly, his lips almost brushing her mouth.

"Only two more days," she answered.

"And then where do you go?" he asked.

"Home, to spend time with my father. How long for you?"

"I think I just extended my stay two more days," he said before brushing his lips over hers.

A thrill shot straight through her. He'd planned on staying. For her. "And then?"

"I have a busy calendar. I'm not sure where my office will send me."

Part of Laney wanted to know everything there was to know about this man she simply knew as Ty, but the other part, the more cautious, no-more-men-in-my-life-thank-you-very-much part of her, was glad she knew next to nothing about him. She'd take away whatever memories they'd make on this island before she headed back to reality and her father's world.

He'd been calling daily, worried sick over her, hoping to coax her home. She'd finally agreed. It was time to stop licking her wounds and face the music and her friends and family. She'd been secreted away far too long, her father pointed out. This was one of the few times, she'd agreed with him.

Laney turned her full attention back to Ty. She knew he had to be quite successful in whatever business he was in. The Wind Breeze Resort only catered to the elite class. Any man who could turn a simple date into a private rooftop dining experience with top-notch entertainment had to have connections, money and power.

But she didn't want to know. She didn't want to get caught up in anything remotely reminiscent of her experience with Justin Overton.

She was happy just to be in Ty's arms, dancing hip to hip with him, feeling his body rub against hers. She'd

instituted a Don't Ask, Don't Tell policy with him and she found she liked it very much.

After several more dances, which had them both incredibly breathless, they left the Top Reef restaurant and when she thought they'd go directly back to the resort, Ty surprised her by driving farther up the coast to a smoky jazz club called Good Sax. Ty had promised to keep her entertained and he was delivering. They sipped cappuccinos and listened to the sensual sounds of a bass saxophone player, Ty sitting next to her, his arm draped around her chair. Every so often he'd nibble on her throat, or stroke the underside of her hair, or take her hand to rub tiny circles over her thumb. The subtle gestures seemed incredibly natural and felt so right but that didn't stop every cell in her body from reacting with raw need. His gentle touches heightened her senses to the point that she didn't think she could take much more without pouncing on him.

She wanted him.

She turned to him and smiled, blinking her eyes, but the words wouldn't come. She wasn't that bold. Not yet.

"Ready to leave?" He didn't wait for her answer. He laid down several bills on the table, rose and took her hand with a look in his eyes that said he knew exactly what she wanted.

And once again, he would deliver.

They almost made love on the hood of his Porsche in the Good Sax parking lot. Ty had whirled around

suddenly when they reached the car, taking her into his arms and kissing her senseless. He touched every part of her body that he could possibly get to without being arrested. And Laney had touched him back, returning his kisses with hot, wet kisses of her own. She ran her hands through his hair, cupped the back of his neck and pressed her body to his.

They came to their senses minutes later when a security guard approached. Laney giggled and straightened her dress while Ty tried to regain his composure below the waist. They drove home in complete silence, Ty knowing better than to touch her as they would surely wind up in a fatal accident. Already Laney was on the path of a major collision, but she didn't care. Living in the moment had its perks, she decided.

Now she stood outside her cottage suite facing Ty, her legs trembling and her heart rate rapidly picking up speed. She'd never wanted a man with such sheer abandon and desire. She wasn't a "party girl" and the tabloids had pretty much left her alone until the wedding fiasco that had splashed negative attention and scandal upon the Royal name. She'd come to the secluded island resort to heal, revamp, unwind and take charge of her life again. Yet, she couldn't imagine saying goodnight to Ty right now. "I don't *ever* do this sort of—"

He bent and kissed the words from her mouth. "Then tell me to leave, Laney," he said quietly, brushing his lips into her hair. "I'll still be here tomorrow, no matter what you decide."

She liked that he gave her the choice, though there really wasn't any other choice she could make. She shoved open the door with her behind, grabbed at his silk tie and tugged him into the room. He breathed a sigh of relief and from that point on, things got a little crazy.

Ty pressed her up against the door and kissed her into oblivion, their tongues mating with openmouthed frenzy. She pulled at his Armani jacket and he struggled out of it while keeping their mouths locked. She undid his tie and he slid her dress down. Before she knew it, she was undressed but for her black thong.

Bare chested and bronzed, Ty bent his head and kissed her breast, then the other, his mouth covering her pebbled tip and sucking her in. A shot of burning heat raced through her.

"You're so beautiful."

Laney thought the same of him. She'd never met a man who'd been so beautiful in body and mind. He seemed to connect with her, even though they knew very little about one another. "Ty," she breathed out. "I want you."

Ty sank down onto his knees. "You'll have me, babe. In a minute. I promise."

Slowly, he lowered her thong down along her thighs, lifting her sandaled feet up one at a time, helping her out of the last piece of her clothing. He planted quick darting kisses up her leg to the juncture of the core, then he touched her there, splaying the folds of sensitive skin, until she let go tiny moans of pleasure, her head thrashing back against the door.

His hands moved up to her torso then, holding her in place at the waist as his mouth covered her, his tongue probing and stroking her inner warmth. She grabbed his thick hair in her hands as he continued to prime her body. The stubble on his face scraped her inner thighs, heightening her awareness even more. When she was ready to combust without him, he stopped, his timing right on.

He rose and lifted her into his arms, kissing her with lips that had just been on her. She felt heady and dizzy and more turned-on than she'd ever been in her life. He strode past the living room, down the hallway to the bedroom and set her onto the bed, quickly removing his pants and briefs. She glimpsed his massive erection right before he sheathed it with a condom. Then he was on the bed, on his back, pulling her on top of him.

She'd never been so daring or felt so exposed.

But Ty's appreciative gaze spurred her courage. "Bold, Laney," he whispered.

She straddled his thighs, fully naked in body and spirit and when he lifted her onto his erection, she sank onto him and he groaned with deep, unabashed pleasure. The sound spurred something wild in her and she moved on him, up and down, riding the tide of his passion. He reached up and touched her arms, her shoulders, guiding her until she found her pace. He cupped her breasts, weighing them with his hands, stroking her nipples with his thumbs.

She rode him hard then, wanting more, wanting all of him. He shoved inside her harder, feeling her need.

And she rode to the brink of her passion climbing to an orgasm that shook her entire body.

Ty watched her release, his eyes grazing hers with intensity and amazingly she didn't feel anything remotely resembling her natural timid nature. With him, she felt open and free.

And then he rolled her over, their bodies and legs entwined and he pushed deeper inside her, his arms braced upon the bed as he reached his climax and thrust into her. Locks of his hair fell forward, perspiration coated his skin and his taut gorgeous body stiffened as he thrust into her one last glorious time, while his gaze pierced deep into her eyes.

Ty bent to kiss her lips before rolling off of her onto his back. "You okay?"

If she were a feline, she'd be purring loudly. "I'm definitely *not* bored."

He caught his breath before rolling to his side, his head braced on his hand. "As promised."

She rolled on her side to face him. "Ty, we don't even know each other's full names."

With his finger, he outlined her lips, swollen now from his passionate kisses. "I figured you wanted it that way."

She debated about a second then nodded. "I do. But how could you know that?"

He shrugged. "Usually a woman asks more questions than a game show host when she meets a man. You didn't ask, because you didn't want any questions in return. I figured you wanted your privacy."

Don't ask, don't tell.

"You're very perceptive." Yet Laney figured she owed him some sort of explanation. After all, they'd just had mind-boggling sex and he'd given her the best lovemaking experience of her life. She wouldn't dwell on the reason for that right now. "I'm not married or…engaged. I mean, I was engaged and it…it didn't work out. I came to the island to forget all about him."

Ty leaned back against the bed and chuckled. "If I helped in any way, I'm glad to be of service."

It wasn't like that. Or was it? Either way, Ty didn't seem the least bit upset about it. "You did. I haven't been thinking much of him lately." Just his betrayal. "But I'm glad I met you." *Whoever you are.*

Laney would never have imagined she'd give herself so fully and completely to a stranger—a hunky mystery man whom she'd never see again after she left the island.

Ty kissed her again and fondled her breasts. "Babe, that goes double for me."

And he gave her an encore performance, *doubling* her pleasure into the night until they exhausted themselves.

Evan finished his shower, taking a thick towel from the shelf in Laney's bathroom and wrapping it around his waist. Finger combing his hair back, he winced in the mirror at his two-day beard. He wasn't exactly on the clock this week, doing some business with pleasure on the island, but the "pirate" look was wearing thin on him.

He needed a shave.

But he needed something else more.

He exited the humid room and walked into the fresh air of the master bedroom where he'd left Laney sleeping. She wasn't in bed any longer.

He found her out on the private lanai overlooking the blue Pacific, on her cell phone. She wore his shirt from last night, the hem barely covering her shapely bottom. He followed the line of her long tanned legs to her bare feet and her white-tipped toenails. Classy.

Something raw tugged at him seeing her wearing his clothes like that.

Ty put on his briefs and trousers, then stepped out onto the balcony watching her body move as she spoke into the cell. He leaned against the French door and listened.

"Yes, I'm feeling a little better now." Laney bobbed her head. "Yes, I know I've been gone almost a month. I miss you, too.

"No, I wasn't aware the problems were escalating, Daddy. I'm sorry I'm not there for you right now."

Laney let go a little sigh. "Of course I'll come home soon. I—I think I'm ready. I love you, too. Very much."

Evan heard the whole conversation including another sigh once she clicked the phone closed. He walked behind her and wrapped his arms around her waist, pulling her tight against him. "Problems?"

She nodded, her blond waves tickling his chin. "It's my father. He runs a big company and things are in chaos."

This was exactly what Evan wanted to hear. He

pushed her hair aside and kissed the back of her neck. "What kind of chaos?"

"Oh, that feels good." She relaxed against his shoulder, fitting into him perfectly before she explained. "He's losing money. It's one mishap after another—fires, mechanical breakdowns, thefts and all kind of things. Now, his blood pressure is up. He wants people around him that he trusts. That means me," she said quietly.

"Go on," he said, "get it all out, babe." Evan continued to nibble on her neck, kissing the soft skin just above her shoulders.

"I think he really needs me. He's getting older and the stress is taking a toll on him. He hasn't been the same since my mother died five years ago. It's been hard on all of us."

"That's understandable," he said, thinking about his own mother and the devastating way his father had died. The memory of that day haunted him still, yet Rebecca Tyler forged on, raising three sons single-handedly. They never had much money growing up, but now she had a good life, living in Florida and enjoying her retirement. Brock, Trent and Evan had developed a successful hotel chain and Tempest had made them multimillionaires within the first four years in operation. Although Rebecca Tyler never asked for anything, her sons made sure she wanted for nothing.

Yet, even knowing that, he couldn't be too unhappy that Nolan Royal's hotels were having trouble.

"How can you help him?"

She shrugged and her beautiful bottom wiggled against him. He was beginning to wish Laney Royal were any other woman. A woman he could pursue once they got back to the mainland.

"I'm not sure I can really. Lately, I've only contributed to his worries instead of helping him. But what he really wants is for me to play a more active role in the business and relieve him of some of the burden."

"And you didn't plan on that?"

Laney shook her head. "No, but I can't afford to break his heart. He doesn't want the company to fail or be sold. He's worked hard all of his life. And now, he wants me by his side, so when the time comes for him to retire, he'll have peace of mind that his legacy will continue."

"And what do you want?"

She beamed with the same kind of passion he'd seen when she got all hot and sexy. "All I want to do is take pictures. I'm a photojournalist at heart. I've sold some of my work to magazines and I want to continue with it. But Dad thinks of it as a hobby. Anything I do outside the business isn't important to him. He doesn't take my work seriously." She made a little hopeless shrug. "I'm all he's got."

She turned around, winding her arms about his neck and resting her pretty eyes on him. "Ty, thanks for listening, but I don't really want to think about my father right now."

Hell, how could he resist that kind of temptation? Evan braced her waist and brought her closer, breath-

ing the sunshine in her hair, whispering into her ear, "I can think of a few ways to distract you."

She ran her fingers along his unshaven beard. "Distract away."

Evan cupped her sweet bottom bringing her up against him and took her in a long lazy slow kiss.

He'd found out what he needed to know for now. There was truth to the rumor that Nolan Royal's hotels were in deep trouble. And that also meant he'd be less of an obstacle when Evan made his move to buy him out. Satisfied with the information he'd garnered, he spent the next part of the morning distracting Laney Royal and enjoying every minute of it.

Later that morning, they took a lazy stroll along the beach, flirting with the waves and each other, playing in the water and sunning themselves until their stomachs grumbled in hunger. Then Ty took Laney to his cottage suite at the opposite end of the Wind Breeze. It was clearly the largest the hotel had to offer. They had a catered lunch on the sundeck and then soaked in the private Jacuzzi.

Laney baked in the sun in the afternoon, Ty being diligent in lathering her with sunscreen, his hands roaming over her body in places the sun would never touch. But after two hours, she needed to rinse off and Ty offered her his shower.

Laney entered the suite's enormous, marble-from-wall-to-floor bathroom, the shower area alone taking up

half the room. Jets from all sides and top streamed down and, before she knew it, Ty entered the shower with only one thing on his mind.

"What do you think about the plumbing in here?" he asked, wearing an innocent expression as he approached in the nude. One thing Laney had learned, there was nothing innocent about Ty, the mystery man. He knew all the right moves and Laney was only too glad to be on the receiving end of his vast knowledge.

She gripped him below the waist, filling her hand with his firm length and returned his innocent look as seven jets rained upon both of them. "I think I've turned everything on properly in here, don't you?"

She slid her hand up and down and Ty growled, the sound echoing against the Italian marble. "Babe, uh, yeah. You've pressed all the right buttons."

Laney loved Ty's sense of humor. It reminded her that she had one of her own. But when he backed her up against the cool marble wall of the shower, all thoughts of humor vanished. Ty had that look in his eyes and Laney knew she was going to be made love to all over again.

In the most delicious way.

They spent the rest of the afternoon in Ty's suite, napping in his bed, eating room-service pizza and drinking beer. Laney beat Ty five games to three in gin rummy and much to her delight, she found out that Ty didn't like to lose, which made teasing him all the more fun.

In the evening they took a moonlit stroll along the beach and then a quick swim in the pool. Laney opened

up a little bit more to Ty about her dilemma with her father. Though she made sure not to reveal too much about her identity, she found talking to him was easy. He listened well and didn't ask too many questions or give his opinion. Who'd have thought the gorgeous stranger wouldn't mind hearing about her love of photojournalism and her lackluster interest in her father's business?

They retired to bed together in Ty's suite and made slow thrilling love to each other. Her body sated, her mind clear, Laney felt hopeful that she could move on from past hurts now. She'd never had a fling before and probably wouldn't have another, but Ty had been exactly what she needed, when she needed it. Besides, how could any fling compare to this one? She'd met the perfect man to help her forget her heartache.

Only a tiny part of her wished for something more with Ty. Or maybe she just wished she'd have more time with him, before having to say goodbye. But, her flight left the island tomorrow evening.

In the morning, Ty woke her early and kissing her quickly, he said, "Get dressed. And bring some layers of clothing with you. Don't forget your camera."

Disheveled and sleep hazy, she asked, "Why, where are we going?"

"To the house of the sun." He patted her butt and tugged at her hair playfully. "Come on, babe. Rise and shine."

By 9:00 a.m., Laney found herself sixty-five feet above sea level at the top of Haleakala Crater, in complete awe of the vista before her. She snapped picture

after picture of the two-million-year-old moonlike crater and the surroundings from the staging area, before the downhill bike ride Ty insisted she shouldn't miss before leaving the island.

He'd been right. Wearing helmets and outer gear to protect against the frigid weather, they sailed down the volcanic crater area on sturdy bikes, dropping to the three-thousand-foot level in less than ten miles, only stopping their exhilarating ride at key lookout points to take amazing pictures. At one point, all five of the islands were visible from where they stood. "This is awesome, Ty. I've never come up here before."

"I thought you'd like it. The landscape's amazing." Then he kissed the tip of her nose. "And the view from where I'm standing isn't half-bad, either."

Laney snapped a candid picture of him then, holding his helmet in hand, wearing a crazy orange jumpsuit, but it was the appreciative look in his eyes that she wanted to capture in time. "I'd have to agree," she said, before putting her helmet back on.

As they biked down closer to sea level, the outer gear came off, Ty giving them up to the driver of the chartered van following them. And once they reached up-country, more level land known for ranches and Hawaiian cowboys, Laney shot more pictures, grateful to Ty for understanding her love of photography and glad to have had this chance.

After leaving Justin at the altar, she'd only snapped pictures of things that required no effort and no research

on her part, her heart too shattered and her confidence too wobbly to make the effort.

But this...this discovery had fulfilled all of her dreams. She knew she'd gotten some great shots today and she had Ty to thank for that.

When they arrived back at the Wind Breeze, Laney realized this would be her last few hours with Ty. She didn't want to waste any time making small talk. She'd seen the hot gleam in his eyes and knew he was thinking the same thing.

They fell onto her bed with great urgency. Hungry mouths, steaming bodies and wild caresses had them panting hard. Ty stroked her to a full climax instantly, knowing her body so well and then she returned the gesture, taking him in her mouth and bringing him to the brink. Ty took control then, positioning her onto her back, lifting her legs to his shoulders and bringing them both to fast and fiery fulfillment in a matter of seconds.

The next time they made love, it was slow, deliberate, a final farewell. Ty took care with her and allowed her the time she needed to come to grips with the end of their weekend together. His kisses were long and lazy and he caressed her body with the tenderness one would lavish on a precious treasure.

Laney was certain she'd never find a better lover. Ty thrilled her, excited her and made her laugh. But he wouldn't make her cry, she told herself. She'd known going into this brief affair, there could be no future for them. She hadn't room in her heart to even try again.

Thanks to Justin Overton, she couldn't put faith in any relationship any time soon. Maybe forever.

So when Ty sat up, glancing at the clock, realizing the time and offering her a ride to the airport, Laney declined.

They'd say their farewells here and now.

Ty kissed her soundly on the lips and gazing at her with regret in his eyes, he said something quite mysterious, like the mystery man that he was. "You were quite a surprise to me, babe."

He left her sitting on the bed, holding a satin sheet to her chest, her hair tousled and wild about her face, wondering exactly what he meant by that.

Three

One month later, Laney bent down on her knees to set a dozen white carnations on her father's grave. He'd always liked the simple traditional flower, sturdy and hearty, a bloom that would thrive a long time. Nolan Royal believed in longevity and in keeping his time-honored namesake hotels first-rate despite the newer, up-and-coming chains. He'd built a prestigious empire on that premise.

Now, the man was gone, but the empire was still alive.

Tears dripped from Laney's eyes as she touched the fresh grass that had been planted over his resting place, as if the caress could possibly bring her closer to him, somehow. "Oh, Daddy," she whispered, "I'm so sorry."

She'd never get over the guilt she felt these past few weeks at not having been stronger for him, not having

been the person he needed, not having helped him more when he seemed to need it most.

When she'd come home from the island after her extended stay, he'd been relieved to see her. He'd been dealing with the tension and pressure of the business failings without her, relying on his right-hand man, the only other person he trusted with inside information, Preston Malloy.

She'd promised her father right before his fatal heart attack that she would work her hardest to help get things back on track. The hotels had been plagued with a run of back luck or worse yet, they'd been deliberately sabotaged.

Her father had been perplexed, angry and frustrated at how so many things could go wrong in such a short span of time. Within months, many of The Royals across the continent had failed in one way or another.

Don't worry, Daddy. I won't disappoint you again. Laney made the vow in her heart and her mind. She was sole beneficiary to The Royal holdings and now everything fell in her lap. She'd assured her father she would keep the hotels thriving and she would do it.

"I'll take care of things now," she promised, staring at her father's bronzed plaque. It rested beside her mother's in a private section of the cemetery.

"I thought I'd find you here." Preston Malloy came up behind her.

She rose from her knees to face him. "What is it?" she asked. "Is there another problem at Royal?"

Preston wrapped an arm around her shoulder and hugged her close. "Not today, Elena."

As close as they'd been through the years, she'd never allowed Preston or anyone besides her mother, father and best friend, to call her Laney. Yet, she'd given her nickname to one other person, on a sandy beach, on an island, at a time in her life when she really needed a friend. Now, those special moments seemed as if they occurred eons ago.

"I just came by to make sure you're okay."

"I'll be fine."

"You've been here every day since the funeral, five days ago."

"I know. I need to feel connected. I want Dad to know I'm here."

"He knows. He wouldn't want you blaming yourself for not being with him when he died. We've already had that talk."

Preston smiled. He was ten years older than her, but he'd become her rock lately, holding up the business end while coordinating all the funeral arrangements. Small wonder that her father valued Preston's abilities and friendship. She was grateful that her father had Preston as his executive assistant. Now, Preston took on another heavy load, dealing with a grieving daughter.

Laney had always suspected her father would have liked to see something happen romantically between the two of them. But though she'd been on several dinner dates with him, nothing had developed in that regard.

"I wish I'd been there to hold his hand during his last moments." Laney shook her head, grief eating at her thinking about her father dying alone.

He'd had an awful day she'd been told, his calendar full of meetings that afternoon. Many believed something or someone had upset him enough to cause his heart to fail. He'd never even made it to the hospital.

Sorrow and wrenching pain filled her with despair. She hadn't gone to work that day, or the days before. Since coming home from Maui, she'd worked diligently beside her father and for the very first time, she'd really gotten a deep sense of the difficulties facing the corporation. Her father hadn't taken the problems well, suspecting there was more than met the eye to these sudden, unexpected setbacks. Seeing the undue stress on her father's face made her dig her heels in, promising him that they'd get to the bottom of the costly hotel mishaps that also had hurt the outstanding Royal reputation.

Laney worked day and night for three solid weeks and had begun to really get into a good stride—until she fainted at work from fatigue. She'd refused medical attention, thinking the long hours and her lack of appetite had contributed to her fainting spell. She'd gone home to rest that day. She thought she would feel better with some rest, but the weakness and fatigue continued. Her father insisted she not come into work until she felt stronger. Three days later, Nolan Royal had gone into cardiac arrest while sitting at his desk and died instantly.

Preston squeezed her shoulders gently. "He always

knew you loved him, Elena. Never fear that. He was very proud of you."

"Was he?" Laney wasn't always so sure. She glanced at his grave and dried her tears with a tissue. "I hope so."

"You know what he'd want right now?"

She shook her head, sadness usurping her thoughts too much to make sense of anything.

"He'd want you to fight for the company. He'd want you to bring The Royals back."

Laney sighed with deep regret. She owed her father that much. She'd put aside her own needs to honor the vow she'd made to him. "I want that now, too, Preston. But I don't know if I can manage it all by myself."

He smiled and kissed her cheek. "You won't have to. You have me."

Laney put down the phone slowly, her head aching, her body stiff with tension. She stared at the paperwork on her late father's desk—which had become her desk now—in the corporate headquarters building adjacent to The Royal Beverly Hills. Sitting in his oversize tufted leather swivel chair, she felt small, diminutive. Her father had been a large man, six feet tall and built like a linebacker. Space was something he valued. His chair, his desk, his office, his dreams were all on a grand scale.

She massaged her forehead and stretched her neck, making head circles to work out the kinks. "A computer glitch in San Diego," she muttered, closing her eyes. The entire reservation system had bleeped off for half a day,

causing The Royals undue losses in potential revenue at the height of the summer season. "What next?" she whispered, tossing her head back against the comfort of the cushioned chair.

When Preston walked into her office, she felt a little better. His dedication had been a godsend these past few weeks. And true to his word at her father's graveside, he'd been right by her side, assisting her in every way he possibly could.

"Is it quitting time?" she asked.

Preston smiled, glancing at his watch, playing along. The day had just barely started. Sunshine streamed into the penthouse office suite bringing morning warmth that hinted at a very hot, humid July day to come. "It could be—you're the boss."

She allowed herself one last moment of relaxation, then leaned forward in the chair, bracing her arms on the desk. "If only," she said, not exactly in jest. She'd been stressed lately and extremely tired, but it was all part of the grieving process, she'd been told. "I've got meetings throughout the day, I could use your input."

Dressed in a light suit coat that fit his form perfectly and made his blue eyes stand out, Preston was the epitome of competence and efficiency. "I heard about the computer glitch in San Diego. I think I need to check it out personally today. I'd planned on being back tomorrow evening."

Inwardly, Laney cringed. Whenever Preston was out of the office, she constantly second-guessed herself.

Having him here to bounce ideas and solutions off, gave her the confidence she needed. Though she worked for Royal before, during and after college, she'd never really taken on a significant role. Suddenly, she was thrust into the driver's seat. "If you think it's necessary."

"I do. We need to find out what caused the problem and make sure it doesn't happen again. It's just two days, but if you'd rather I didn't go—"

"No, no. You should go. I'll hold down the fort."

Preston nodded. "Okay, but have dinner with me tomorrow night. You look like you could use a break."

Dinner? She hesitated. He'd been rather obvious about his desire to date her a few years ago and she didn't want to encourage anything again. The last thing she needed now was to complicate her life at the moment. "I'm not eating much these days, Preston."

He cast her a warm, encouraging smile. "Your father wouldn't want you to be alone so much. Besides, I should *make* you eat something. You gave us all a scare when you fainted that day."

"I won't faint again."

"Darn right. Because we're going to have a nice peaceful meal tomorrow night and I'll fill you in on my findings from my trip."

"Okay," she agreed, finally. She was being foolish. Preston was only looking out for her welfare and they did have to spend time together after hours some of the time until Laney felt more confident about her position here. "Call me when you get back tomorrow."

"I will," he said, satisfied. "I'm off now. You know how to reach me if you need anything."

Laney watched him leave, closing the door behind him. When her cell phone rang, she glanced at the number and immediately answered. "Julia, thank God. Your timing is perfect. I need my best friend right now."

"Oh, Laney, I think I sensed it. We haven't spoken much this week. How're you doing? Still not eating?"

"I can't. My stomach's not right. It's from all the stress I'm sure. And believe me, you can cut the tension with a knife around here. The employees aren't thrilled at having me take up where my father left off. Most of them think they know more than me. And guess what, they just might."

Julia chuckled, the same girlish laugh she remembered when they went to private school together. "No, they don't. They're just used to taking orders from your father. Don't let them push you around."

"Many of them were working here when I'd come around selling candy bars for school fund-raisers. It's hard to gain their respect. But I am my father's daughter. I'll prove to them I know what I'm doing. It's just going to take a little while." Laney hoped so, anyway. She'd gotten a degree in business and had a good background, but she'd been thrust at the helm so suddenly, while still reeling from a broken engagement and her father's death. Yet, she was the go-to person. The buck stopped with her. "I'm managing, Julia."

"I know you are. Your father would be proud."

Laney sighed with relief. "Thanks, hon. You always know how to cheer me up."

"I've got another cheer or two in me. Our days at SC weren't that long ago." Laney flashed an image of the two of them at USC, cheering for the Trojans. Both had crushes on the quarterback. "So let me take you to lunch today."

Laney groaned. The mention of food brought queasiness to her stomach. "Why does everyone try to feed me?"

"Because we're worried about you. I've been over at your place enough lately to see what you're eating, which is next to nothing. Are you sure you're fine?"

"I'm…doing…okay."

"I know that tone, best girlfriend. You are not *okay*."

"It's just all this turmoil in my life. Really, I appreciate the offer, but I'm not taking lunches these days." Laney wouldn't admit to Julia that maybe something more was wrong with her. She didn't want to worry her best friend. Her suspicions were unfounded at the moment. She'd been through a world of grief and upheaval in her life lately. That had to be the reason she didn't feel quite like herself.

"Okay, then, but I'm holding you to lunch this weekend. You need to get away from the office, get your mind off business. We'll go down to the beach and have a peaceful meal, clear your head."

"Sounds great," she answered truthfully. Julia was the one person who really understood her. Spending time with her always helped her forget her problems. "I'm looking forward to it." She hung up the phone feeling much better.

* * *

An hour later, Laney looked up from the pile of reports on her desk when someone knocked briskly on the office door. Before she could acknowledge the knock, the door pushed open and a man strode into the room.

Laney rose immediately, startled.

"Hello, Laney."

Ty? Her mystery man was here, standing in her office? Laney swallowed and stared in disbelief. That deep, sensual voice reminded her of romantic nights and sizzling sex. Her first thought was: he looked gorgeous. Her second: she was overjoyed seeing him. She hadn't forgotten the glorious days they'd spent together last month. Alone in her Brentwood home at night, thoughts of him would filter in and she'd smile at the memory of her steamy, hot, short-lived fling. She'd never done anything quite so spontaneous or been so uninhibited as she'd been with him. He had helped her through a very bleak time in her life.

"Ty." She drank in the sight of him, dressed in a black suit, with the collar opened at the throat. She remembered nibbling on that throat and gaining his undivided attention. She couldn't keep a wide smile from emerging. "What are you doing here?"

"I came to see you."

"But how did you know where to find me?"

He smiled slowly as he approached. She stepped away from the desk to stand a few feet from him, her heart racing. She stared into his eyes. And he stared

back. That familiar gleam was there, the one that told her he appreciated what was before his eyes. "I'll explain that later. How are you?"

"I'm…I'm…stunned, actually. I never thought I'd see you again."

Ty nodded and closed the gap between them. He took her hand. His touch sent tingles from her palm clear up her arm. He closed his fingers around hers, drew her close and brushed a soft, exquisite kiss on her lips.

Laney responded instantly, savoring his warm lips on her, the familiar scent that could heat her instantly. She kissed him back with full abandon and was left breathless when their mouths broke apart. But when he looked into her eyes, regret marred his expression. "I didn't really plan on it happening this way. I heard about your father."

Laney's eyebrows shot straight up. "You know my father? How?"

"I'm sorry, Elena." Her secretary barged in. "I stepped away from my desk for a moment."

"No, no. It's okay, Ally." She took her eyes off Ty to give a direct order to her secretary. "Hold my calls. And please tell my ten o'clock appointment I'm running a little late."

"But, he *is* your ten o'clock appointment." Ally glanced at Ty, puzzled.

"Don't be silly," she said. "He doesn't have a…" Then she walked over to the appointment book sitting on her desk, just to double-check. She'd known about her ten o'clock, dreading the meeting. She'd seen his

name on the schedule this morning and immediately her stomach had clenched. "Just tell Evan Tyler to wait."

She'd like to keep that man waiting until hell froze over. He'd been a thorn in the Royals' side and had added to her father's stress level over the months, advocating a buyout of the chain. When she found out he'd been the last appointment on the books before her father's fatal heart attack, Laney knew she'd have to face him one day.

Today, was the day.

And she'd wished that she'd asked Preston to stay for that appointment. Laney had suspected the man capable of aggravating her father enough to send him into cardiac arrest. But thankfully, she'd gotten a short reprieve when Ty entered the room.

"Uh, Elena?"

"Ally, what is it?"

"I'll straighten this out." Ty turned to face her secretary. "You can go back to your desk now, Ally. Miss Royal doesn't need you at the moment."

Ally peered over Ty's shoulder, her eyes wide with desperate concern.

"It's…fine," Laney said, trying to ease Ally's alarm, but Ty had already ushered her secretary out of the room. Laney had never heard that tone in Ty's voice before, or seen this commanding side of him.

"Ty?"

Then it struck her. Like a giant oak toppling onto her head. Or should she say, a tall palm tree, from the

island. Ty…Tyler? Ty, her mystery man, was of course, Evan Tyler. They were one and the same! Laney closed her eyes as impending dread crept in. "Oh, no! Tell me it's not true."

She opened her eyes. Ty stared at her. "I'm your ten o'clock appointment, babe."

Laney backed up, shaking her head, her body trembling. "Babe," she repeated, quietly stunned. "*Babe?* Are you kidding me? You're Evan Tyler! You're… you're… Oh, God!"

He just stood there, watching her meltdown. She shook so violently now, she had to brace herself against her desk. Then she gave up trying to stand on legs that would surely buckle under her. She plopped into her chair, the desk protecting her from Evan Tyler, the man responsible for her father's heart attack. She was certain of it now.

"You coldhearted bastard."

"Laney, listen—"

"You took advantage of me. Of my situation. And I played right into your hands, didn't I?"

As the shock wore off, fury filled her. Fueled with anger she rose from the chair, refusing to submit to the scoundrel another second. She faced him head-on. "You used me in the worst possible way! You did, didn't you? Tell me the truth, if you have it in you. You knew who I was the whole time at the Wind Breeze, didn't you?"

Evan Tyler's lips hardened into thin lines. "I knew."

Laney wanted to throw the Waterford vase on the

desk at him. She wanted to knock him out and drag him from her office from the pain he caused her. Everything inside burned with humiliation. She'd been duped, fooled by an unfeeling, hard-nosed deceiver. And what really ticked her off, aside from having slept with the enemy, was that he'd destroyed the only true good memory she'd had to hold on to during her time of mourning. "Damn you. I'd heard of your ruthless reputation, but this has to be one that would make it into the Guinness book."

Evan Tyler didn't argue the point. He didn't apologize for anything, either.

"I came here to offer my condolences."

Laney jammed her arms across her middle, holding her temper hostage for a moment. "You do know that you were the last person to see my father alive."

"That's debatable, Laney."

"You caused his heart attack!"

"Like hell I did. When I walked out of his office, he was smiling. He'd blown me off in a matter of ten minutes and he was glad to do it."

"You're lying. Don't try to deny it. You told him about sleeping with me, didn't you? That was part of the plan, wasn't it? You wanted to buy him out and you'd stoop to hitting below the belt to do it. You'd use any means to get what you wanted."

"Your father wasn't a saint, Laney. He cheated me out of a deal I'd worked on for two years. I wasn't feeling overly generous toward any Royal when I saw

you at the Wind Breeze bar, drinking away your sorrows. When you didn't recognize me, I figured, what the hell. You were beautiful and lonely and looking at me like I was the last man on earth."

"You're modest, too, I see." Laney blinked away that vivid memory. It was true. She must have looked like a little lost lamb, just waiting to be slaughtered by the big bad wolf, and Evan Tyler charged in for the kill, right on schedule. Oh, she'd been such a fool.

He ignored her gibe. "My original plan was to rub Nolan's nose in the fact we'd been together on the island. But, no, he never knew. I didn't tell him."

"And I'm supposed to believe you?"

"It's the truth." He stood firm.

"You wanted to rattle his cage. Weaken the enemy. Right? So, if I'm to believe you, which I don't, what would have changed your mind?"

Evan looked into her eyes. Then he glanced at her mouth. At one time, his direct appreciation, the hot look in his eyes, would've heated her body to smoldering. But now all she felt was disdain.

"You. You changed my mind."

She shook her head. "I'll never believe that."

He didn't try to convince her. "I'm in the hotel business. I knew about the problems at Royal. Anyone doing an ounce of research would know that the hotels were having problems."

"But that didn't stop you from questioning me."

"You volunteered the information."

"You seduced it out of me!"

Evan's dark eyes took on a hard gleam. "I never heard you complain."

Laney closed her eyes briefly, fighting for control of her fury. "You had an agenda. You used me to get information. I was your ace in the hole, the weapon you planned to use against my father."

"Listen, you only confirmed my suspicions about Royal. I'll admit that. But you can't deny we had a good time on the island."

Laney didn't want to think about being with him on the island. She was certain every word that came out of his mouth was an out-and-out lie. "I can't recall. I've blocked out those memories."

Ty scoffed at that, his mouth twisting into a crooked smile. "Now who's lying?"

Laney calmed herself. She took in oxygen and sat at her desk, keeping her chin held high, refusing to give him any more satisfaction than she already had. When her head continued to throb, she sighed with impatience. "What do you want?"

Evan took a seat across the desk from hers. "I want what I've always wanted. To buy out The Royals."

"No. Meeting over. You may show yourself out."

"You're not cut out to run this company."

"Don't tell me what I can or can't do, Mr. Tyler."

"Damn it, Laney. I've seen you naked half a dozen times. Call me Evan."

Laney inhaled sharply and frowned. "So kind of you

to remind me. But it doesn't change anything. I'll never sell the company."

"It's in trouble, Laney. You know it and I know it. Your father couldn't fix it and I doubt you'd get even close. It's not a reflection on you personally. It's just plain fact." He stood then, his shoulders broad, his eyes focused on hers and she met his stare with a hard one of her own. She disregarded his handsome face and the truth to his claims. "Don't be a fool, Laney. The hotels are losing money. They'll go under if you don't do something soon. I'm offering you a way to save them."

"My answer is no."

Evan shook his head as if she were a schoolgirl misunderstanding an easy mathematical problem. "I'm leaving my offer on the table. I'll be back." He strode to the door, then turned to meet her stare, an unexpected earnest look in his eyes. "And just for the record, I remember *everything* about the island."

Four

Laney watched Julia scoop up a pile of fries and wolf them down one by one without blinking. They sat at a seaside café on Saturday afternoon. Her stomach squeezing tight, Laney looked at her veggie sandwich and wondered if she could manage it.

"You haven't taken a bite yet, Laney." Julia picked up her patty melt oozing with Cheddar cheese and finished it off. "And I'm all done. You'd think I was eating for two." She laughed. "Me and you."

Laney closed her eyes briefly and put a hand to her stomach. "No, you're not eating for two. I am." She glanced at her friend and tried to smile.

Julia's face paled. She put the down the Diet Coke she was about to sip. "W-What?"

Laney pushed her plate aside. "I think I'm pregnant, Jules."

Shock registered on Julia's face, which she tried very sweetly to hide. She leaned forward and lowered her voice. "You *think* you're pregnant, but you're not sure?"

"I have all the symptoms. I've never felt like this before. Not even when I ran away from the wedding and Justin. The queasiness, the lack of appetite, and there's the fact that I missed my period. I made an appointment with my doctor for next week."

"Oh, I thought you and Justin had decided to, uh, refrain, before the wedding. Are you going to tell him?"

Laney shook her head. She abhorred thinking about Justin. She hadn't had sex with him in the weeks prior to the wedding. She'd been so busy with the final arrangements, the wedding planner and spending time with her bridesmaids, that she and Justin had decided to spend their last few weeks apart before the ceremony.

Now, Laney could add Evan Tyler to her list of men she'd rather forget. Both men had deceived her. She popped a Tums in her mouth. It helped with her shaky stomach and other rocky emotions. "I would, if it were his baby."

This time, poor Julia couldn't hide her shock. Her sculpted auburn brows rose, making four crinkle lines appear in her forehead. Lines, she'd normally go to great lengths to avoid creating. Julia opened her mouth, but no words came forth.

"It's pretty bad, I'm afraid." Then Laney unloaded

the entire story to her friend about her time at the Wind Breeze Resort and the mystery man who'd turned out to be a scoundrel and her father's competitor. She left nothing out. A lifelong friendship meant spilling it all, even the smallest of details.

"Oh, wow." Julia gazed out to the Pacific Ocean trying to come up with something positive to say, Laney presumed. But they both knew this was as hopeless, as hopeless could get.

"I know. Believe me, I'm just as shocked. We used protection."

"So, what happened? I mean, *how* did it happen?"

"Well, there was this one time, in the shower…and, damn it, we really were careful all the other times."

Julia sank deeper into the tall wicker throne seat, her arms braced on the rests. This had always been their favorite beachside café. As young girls, they'd lean back and pretend they were island queens—eating lavish foods, sipping exotic drinks, with the world at their feet—and share their innermost secrets. Now, Laney was grateful she had Julia to confide in and that part in her life hadn't changed.

"Why didn't you tell me all this the minute you got back from Maui?"

"I don't know." She ducked her head slightly. "I'm sorry. It's just with everything happening at once at Royal and then my father dying, I just couldn't bring myself to share this. It seemed…trivial and self-indulgent." Her time with "Ty" the mystery man, had

been anything but trivial. It had been glorious. But it hadn't been real—none of it.

"No one would ever describe you as self-indulgent, Laney. You wanted to hold on to those few good memories, and after what you'd been through with Justin, I can understand that. So, what are you planning to do now?"

"Nothing. I'm not going to do a thing."

Julia blinked. "Oh-kay."

"I can't deal with this right now. I have a company to run. I have to keep focused. I can't let—"

"You might have a baby to think about, honey. That's important, too."

"I know. I'll take care of the baby." Laney patted her stomach with a protective hand. If she were pregnant, she couldn't fault the new life growing inside her. The child was innocent and would receive all the love she had to give. "I'm coming to terms with that. I'll love this child. Believe me. I've always wanted children."

"Oh, I know you will. There was never any doubt about that, but what about the father?"

"I really can't stand thinking about him. He most likely caused my father's heart attack. He's about as heartless as they come. I'll deal with him later when the situation forces me to come to a decision."

Julia nodded in agreement. Thankfully, she had her best friend's support in that.

"Right now, no one knows but you and me. I'd like to keep it that way."

Julia's lips lifted as she reached for her hand. "Laney, that's what we always do. Keep each other's secrets. But when the time comes, I get to throw you the biggest baby shower. Promise?"

"Promise." Laney leaned back in her Queen of the Island chair, closing her eyes and thanking heaven for best friends.

Later that week, Laney rubbed her tension-filled forehead just as Preston Malloy walked into her office. "Preston, please close the door."

She waited until he sat before sharing the news. "I just received word that there's been a flood at The Royal Phoenix."

"How bad is it?" he asked with a calm that Laney wished she could absorb into her own chaotic life. Preston had a good head for business and had become her life preserver in the face of very choppy waters. Over their business dinner the other night, he reassured her that the San Diego computer glitch wouldn't happen again. He'd taken additional, but costly measures to see that they had a backup reservation system for all the hotels. Laney had approved the requisition immediately.

"It's bad. The entire first floor just had renovations. All the new carpeting and furniture was involved. I need you to check to see if we're covered by insurance. You might have a fight on your hands. The insurance company hasn't been too happy with all the claims

we've filed this year. The Phoenix manager says a faulty pipe burst during the night. That's all I know right now."

"Okay, I'll check into it."

"We'll have to scramble now to get the lobby and reservation desk operating again somehow. You know how proud my father was of that main lobby. He'd commissioned sculptures and artwork personally to suit that location. I'm praying none of that art was destroyed."

Preston rose instantly. "Don't worry, Elena. I'll take care of it. Will you be around this afternoon?"

Laney sighed. "No, I have an appointment with…well, it's something I can't neglect. Trust me, I wouldn't leave you with this mess if it wasn't very important."

Preston smiled. "I'll handle it. You can count on me."

"I do," she said in earnest. "But call me if you find out anything more about Phoenix, okay? You can reach me at home tonight."

"I'll be sure to do that," he said as he turned to leave. Then he swung back around to add, "I had a nice time at dinner the other night, Elena."

"Me, too."

"And just for the record, you're doing an excellent job here at Royal."

"Thank you," Laney said, grateful for Preston's constant support. She wished she could feel the same way, but in fact, Laney felt as though the entire hotel chain were crumbling around her feet.

Three hours later, Laney's mood had gone from bad to worse. She'd visited her ob-gyn and he had con-

firmed her suspicions: the recent pregnancy tests she'd taken at home weren't false positives. She was six weeks pregnant. That meant Evan Tyler was the father of her baby.

She drove down the 405 Interstate in a state of shock. She thought she had a handle on this and fully expected that her suspicions had been correct, but when the doctor announced, "You're pregnant," the full impact of her situation struck her with stunning force. The baby was due next spring. *Her* baby. The reality that in less than eight months, she'd be holding her own little helpless child in her arms, struck her anew.

She was really pregnant.

A life for a life, her father would say.

It was strange how true that was in her case. Just weeks before her father died, Laney had conceived a child. And even stranger yet was that Nolan Royal would never know his grandchild because Evan Tyler, the baby's father, might very well also be responsible for his death.

Tears welled in her eyes. She wiped them quickly to clear her vision, but she couldn't wipe away the searing pain of losing her father. "I miss you, Daddy," she whispered quietly, her hands rigid on the steering wheel. He may not have been a perfect father. He'd expected so much from her, but he'd also loved her very much. It was as if when her mother died, he'd thrust all of the love he'd had for her mother onto Laney. And he'd looked to Laney for that same kind of devotion.

Both her mother and father were gone now and the dawning knowledge that she was alone in the world but for some distant relatives, brought agonizing sadness.

When her queasy stomach grumbled with hunger she was reminded that she wasn't really alone. A baby grew inside her. She smiled at the thought. Regardless of all else, she would love this child. The two of them would be a family.

Laney got off the freeway at Sunset Blvd. and drove home, ready to soak in a hot tub and then try to eat something. The doctor had warned her about staying healthy in body and mind. She needed nourishment. He'd offered her a prescription for her nausea, but Laney hated taking medication so she hadn't swallowed one pill yet. She wanted to try to conquer the queasiness on her own.

She hit the remote to her garage and pulled her car inside, just as another car pulled up in her driveway. She got out of her car, closing the door, curious about the shining silver sports car that had appeared out of nowhere.

She walked to the edge of the garage, squinting in the afternoon sun as a man stepped out of the car wearing faded jeans and a white cotton shirt with the sleeves rolled up.

For a second her heart raced—memories of casual walks on a Hawaiian beach with a handsome stranger kicked in. Laney glanced at his pant legs when he strode up the driveway. Staring curiously, her throat tight and dry, she barely managed, "Boots?"

"Born in Texas."

Laney nodded, as if that made all the sense in the world, but it had shown her just how little she'd really known about the man she'd once called Ty.

"Did you follow me?" she asked, puzzled. She'd put nothing past him.

"No. Just good timing."

"That's debatable. We have nothing to say to each other, Mr. Tyler." She wouldn't ask how he'd found out her private home address. A man like Evan Tyler had ways to get the information he needed. Hadn't she learned that brutal lesson, firsthand?

He twisted his mouth. "Mr. Tyler again?"

She'd ticked him off and took childish satisfaction in that. "I'm not going to allow you to buy Royal out, so please, get off my property."

"You need to listen to reason, Laney. Take a drive with me. We'll go somewhere peaceful and talk."

Laney wanted to put a protective hand to her trembling stomach, but she didn't dare. And she couldn't quite block out the doctor's routine inquiries today about the baby's father—health history questions she couldn't answer. Laney would have to get those answers soon.

Once again, she fought off tears. "Evan, please leave me alone."

"You're emotional right now, but—"

"Damn right, I'm emotional. My father just died! And you were the last person to see him alive. If you don't think that makes me emotional and sorry I ever laid on eyes on you—"

"Hey! Calm down."

Evan closed the gap between them. He kept his hands to himself, thankfully. If he touched her, she feared she'd melt into a puddle of tears. Her emotions were that close to the edge.

"What's wrong with you?"

"I just told you."

"No, it's something else. You're pale as a ghost."

"You have that effect on me."

Evan lips pursed tight. "Laney, come on. Don't be ridiculous."

"I'm not being ridiculous. I want to know exactly what you said to my father that day."

"And I want to speak with you about The Royals. Seems we both want something. Since now isn't a good time for you, have dinner with me tomorrow night and I'll answer all of your questions."

Laney hesitated. Her stomach clenched. She was finally hungry, which didn't happen often these days. She needed a peaceful meal and a nice warm bath. Then she planned on crawling into bed. What she didn't want to do was have an emotional breakdown in front of Evan Tyler. She couldn't let him see her that way. She wasn't ready to tell him about the baby, but she desperately did need to find out if he had anything to do with her father's heart attack. "Okay, fine. I'll meet you for a quick business dinner."

He shook his head. "I'll pick you up at eight, tomorrow night right here. And I won't be wearing my boots."

Laney watched him drive off as myriad emotions swam around in her head. Flashes of the man she'd known at the Wind Breeze wouldn't stop infiltrating her thoughts. She'd caught rare glimpses of that man when he glanced at her. She'd only wished he were half the man she'd known on that island. But at best, he was a coldhearted driven businessman out to raid her father's hard-earned company.

"Well, baby," she whispered, as her stomach growled with hunger again. "That was your daddy."

Evan drove into the underground garage at the L.A. Tempest and parked the car in his personal space, his mind focused solely on Laney Royal. When he should be thinking about ways to get her to sign on the dotted line, all he really could focus on was how he could get her back in his bed.

There was just something surprising about the beautiful Miss Royal. Maybe it was the challenge she represented to him. He wanted her company, but after spending time with her, he found he wouldn't mind any fringe benefits that came along with the deal. She'd managed to cure his own boredom at the Wind Breeze, breaking up his business routine and allowing him to enjoy moments of sheer relaxation. And when they weren't relaxing they were hot for each other, tangling in and out of the sheets. He squeezed the vision of her smooth, supple body under his out of his head before his pulse escalated and his temperature rose. Every time

he thought of her that way, his body surged like a damn power strip in a blackout.

Hell, she clearly couldn't stand the sight of him. She believed that he had something to do with the death of her father.

Evan clicked off the ignition, grabbed his briefcase and slid out of the car, slamming the door. He rode the private elevator up to his penthouse apartment, angry that she'd believe him of aggravating her father into cardiac arrest.

He was still in a mood when he unlocked his door and was greeted by his mother and two brothers.

They stood in the afternoon shade on his courtyard balcony, with champagne glasses in hand. His mother smiled warmly, her brown eyes twinkling, while his two brothers barely held back smirks.

He glared at his brothers then ran a hand down his face. "Amazing who the doorman lets in these days." Then Evan walked over to his mother. "I didn't mean you," he said with a wink. He bent to give her a kiss. "It's always good to see you, Mom."

"Your brothers flew me in from St. Petersburg to surprise you. Did you forget your own birthday, Evan?" she asked, her expression bordering on grim.

"I've been busy, Mom. I thought we agreed to celebrate next month in Florida when you hit the big—"

"Don't say it," Trent warned.

Brock walked over to hand him a glass of champagne. "You're taking your life in your hands."

Rebecca Tyler waved off her boys. "Oh, pooh! I'm not ashamed to admit I'll be sixty years old next month and you boys know that. But your birthday is today, Evan. I hear you're working very hard."

"I'm putting together a deal that'll put Tempest in a whole different league."

Rebecca blinked and nodded, then she took a seat on a chaise lounge, looking a bit weary. The three of them took their cue from her and sat, circling her seat. "You've already made me so proud. All three of you boys. You've got a thriving business with Tempest. I was just hoping…"

She let the sentence drop, but they all knew what she was thinking. Evan glanced at Brock, who glanced at Trent, and neither one of them wanted to look their mother directly in the eyes.

Trent spoke up first. "How old are you today, Ev, thirty-three?"

Evan twisted his mouth. "If you say so."

"Trent, you know your brother is thirty-*two*. All of my sons are two years apart."

"Yeah, but Ev's the oldest," Brock said and it was beginning to sound the way it had when they'd been kids, pointing fingers and laying blame.

His mother raised her glass. "To Evan. My oldest son. Happy Birthday, dear."

Brock and Trent chorused the birthday sentiment and they each raised their glass and sipped champagne.

"I remember the day you were born. It didn't seem

so long ago," she said, her eyes taking on a distant gleam. Often she appeared that way when she thought of times when their father had been alive. "You gave me the most trouble before you were born. I was nauseous every morning for months, barely had any appetite at all. The doctors worried about me losing weight. They didn't have those nausea pills like they have now. But you were my easiest delivery." His mother sighed. "And now you're the head of a big company." She sipped her drink then smiled wistfully. "Did I tell you Larissa Brown's daughter is having another baby and her son is getting married this fall?"

"I don't think we knew that," Brock said, "did we, Ev?"

Evan shook his head and kept his mouth shut. "Nope." He knew better than to engage in a conversation with his mother about marriage and babies. She'd been hinting for years. He couldn't say he blamed her. She had three sons, all of age and not a one of them was remotely interested in settling down.

"Hey, Mom, I hear you're finally going on a cruise," Trent said, changing the subject.

"Yes, Larissa convinced me to go with her. She says I don't know what I'm missing—all those activities and tours. We're leaving in two weeks. I'm getting things packed and ready."

Trent continued asking about his mother's vacation, giving Evan the best birthday gift of all: a reprieve from his mother's subtle hints. He'd never minded being the oldest, bearing the burden of helping her raise Trent and

Brock, but now Rebecca Tyler wanted more in life. And she looked to Evan to get the ball rolling.

Later that evening they dined at The Palm, a well-established Los Angeles restaurant known for their specialty of the house—jumbo Nova Scotia lobsters—to celebrate Evan's birthday. It was his mother's favorite place to eat when in L.A. Caricatures of famous celebrities who'd frequented the restaurant were painted on the walls and every time Rebecca came in, his mother would find several new cartoons drawn onto the "living murals."

It was just the four of them and Evan liked it that way. He wasn't one for big parties and displays. That was more Brock's style. He and Trent ran the Tempest Hotels in Texas, New Mexico, Colorado and Arizona while Evan kept control of all their California hotels from San Diego to Hollywood to San Francisco. He was also in charge of acquisitions, being the better negotiator of the three. Soon, they'd add the Maui Paradise hotel to their chain.

But Evan wanted more. He wanted The Royals. If he could acquire them in a deal with Laney Royal, not only would Tempest stand to gain more widespread national appeal, but they would have knocked out their biggest competitor. He'd just have to make sure Laney saw things his way tomorrow night.

Actually, he couldn't wait for the challenge.

Five

Laney pulled her hair back and secured it with a barrette at the nape of her neck. She put on a black suit, a fitted blazer and skirt that screamed all business, no pleasure. She wore little jewelry, but for the diamond stud earrings that had been her mother's. She'd treat this dinner with Evan as business as usual and nothing more.

That was the plan until she answered the knock on her front door precisely at eight o'clock to find Evan standing there, looking like every woman's fantasy. Dressed in slate gray, wearing an Italian cut suit, his dark hair groomed and combed back with just a hint of stubble on his face, and no cowboy boots to be found, he earned an admiring stare from Laney.

"It's good to see you, Laney." He said it as if he meant

it. A shiver of sexual awareness shimmied through her body. She peered over his shoulder to the jet-black limousine waiting. She realized she'd grossly underdressed for whatever Evan had in mind, and normally the fashion faux pas would have plagued her all evening. But tonight she decided to turn the tables on him.

"I think I would have preferred cowboy boots, Evan."

He took no offense, but only laughed. "Then let's just make a quick stop to my penthouse and—"

"No, thank you," she said quickly. "I want to remind you, this is a business dinner."

Evan studied her hair and the blond waves she'd tucked safely into a sterling silver prison. His gaze traveled to her face, meeting her eyes with a slow searing look before lowering to her lips. Laney's heart beat harder. Her head swam as he scrutinized her mouth. And when he dipped his gaze lower yet to scan her buttoned lace blouse and the hint of cleavage Laney couldn't hide, she had to warn herself to be careful. He wasn't to be trusted.

"You look beautiful."

"I wasn't going for *beautiful*."

"I know. You can't help it."

His compliment shot straight to her head, like a brain freeze after sipping an ice-cold chocolate malt too quickly. But Laney rebelled against it. She retreated back in her doorway. "This isn't a good idea."

Evan reached for her hand, wrapping his fingers over hers. "It's a very good idea." He softened his tone.

"You're working too hard. Take a break. Let's have a quiet meal and talk."

She hated that his touch, the soothing way his hand covered hers, didn't repel her. Or that the sound of his voice only brought familiar, fond memories. She wouldn't be fooled again, but she did need answers from him.

Her stomach was back on the blink. She'd barely eaten a bite today, the thought of food making her sick. She only hoped she could make it through dinner tonight with him.

"Okay, fine." She released herself from his grasp and locked up her house. "Let's get this over with."

Evan set a hand to her back guiding her to the limousine, waving off his chauffeur and opening the door for her himself. She settled into the backseat as he closed the door.

Before she knew it, they'd traveled to the beach and headed north up the coastline.

"You ready for some wine? Champagne?"

She looked at the fully stocked bar again, then up at him. "No, thank you. I'm not celebrating anything."

He leaned back against the cushiony leather seat. "At one time, you didn't need a reason to have a drink with me."

"That *wasn't* you, Evan."

"No? How can you be so sure?"

"I'm sure," she said rather smugly, proud that she'd managed to put a frown on his face.

"You know, you don't need to cover yourself up in a

prim business suit. I know what's underneath. And I'm not just speaking about your sexy body."

"Sure, say that now while the car is traveling at sixty miles an hour and I can't jump out."

Evan let go a deep chuckle. "Smart-ass."

All in all, Laney was pretty darn proud of herself for holding her own with the likes of ruthless, driven, gorgeous, Evan Tyler.

In her estimation, he was no better than Justin Overton. Both men had hurt her, but Evan had the distinction of possibly being responsible for her father's heart attack. And while he was her baby's father, he was also her enemy, a man she would never trust.

Originally, Evan wanted to hate Laney Royal. She was the spoiled, wealthy, indulged daughter of Nolan Royal. How could she be anything else? But he'd found her remarkably unlike her father, which had been a genuine surprise. The woman with the hot little body and pretty sky-blue eyes had wit and humor and brains to match. In his quest to extract information from her, he'd found that he'd enjoyed the time he spent with her on the island.

He wanted her hotels and she couldn't stand the sight of him. She looked at him as if a monstrous blast of fire would spew out his mouth any second. But she was far from a withering damsel in distress. That made what he was about to do very tricky. He'd tried speaking to her rational side without success, so tonight he'd have to speak to her emotions.

When they reached the seaside restaurant, Evan took Laney's hand and led her inside. They were immediately shown to an intimate corner table he'd reserved for the night.

"I hope this meets with your approval," Bradley, the maître d', said.

"This is perfect. Thank you."

Oysters on the half shell and a bottle of fine red wine awaited them. Outside spotlights shimmered on the shoreline, illuminating crashing waves upon the sand. Stars glimmered above. Warm summer air filtered in through the expanse of open French doors lining the back of the restaurant.

"This is very nice, Evan. But hardly a place to conduct business."

Evan smiled. "Let me worry about that."

He poured her a glass of wine and then one for himself. Color drained from Laney's face the minute she glanced at the oysters.

"What's wrong? I know you love oysters. We had our share of them—"

"Stop!" She put up a hand and closed her eyes. "I'd appreciate you not reminding me about anything I said or did on Maui. Okay?"

He narrowed his eyes. What was up with her? "What are you afraid of, Laney?"

"Can we get just get down to business," she said, pushing aside her glass of wine and the decorative plate of oysters, without giving them so much as another glance.

"Before we order? Sorry, babe, but I'm hungry. We'll talk business after the meal."

When the waiter came by, he appeared genuinely concerned. "Is there something wrong with the wine, Mr. Tyler? Or the oysters? I can assure you they're the finest quality—"

"No, no, everything's great. The table is just as I arranged." Evan sipped from his glass of wine to appease him. "I think we're ready to order now."

The waiter put on a smile and began reciting the nightly specials. Evan listened, darting quick glances Laney's way. Her face paled even more when the waiter began describing the fare in great detail.

"If you'll allow me to order," Evan said, looking at Laney with keen interest now, "their grilled swordfish is the best—"

"I'll just have a salad, Evan." She cast him a small smile.

"Salad?" Evan scratched his head. The waiter jerked back, appearing slightly insulted.

"If I might suggest the jumbo Cajun prawn salad with lobster dressing," the waiter offered.

Laney's eyes widened and she shook her head. "Please, just a green salad with no dressing."

Evan glanced at the waiter. "Bring us two swordfish dinners. I'll see if I can't get the lady to change her mind."

"Yes, sir."

"Tell me you're not on a diet." Evan said, once the waiter was out of hearing distance.

Laney glanced out the French doors appearing extremely interested in the shoreline. "No, but I'm not very hungry."

"You've lost weight, Laney. Not that you don't look good, but you're—"

"Stress, Evan. Okay? I said it. I'm under a good deal of stress lately."

Evan sipped his drink. "That's why I'm here. To wipe away all your stress."

"You only add to it," she said quietly.

"Have some wine. It'll relax you."

Laney glanced at the goblet filled two-thirds full of rich red wine. "I'm not... I'm not..."

Tears built up in her eyes. She tried valiantly to hide them, but Evan noticed and something powerful tugged at his heart. "Laney, listen. No more jabbing at each other. Your hotels are sinking fast. I know more than you think I know about your problems. Get out while you can. While they're still worth something."

"It's not that bad, Evan. You're making the situation out to be worse than it is."

"Maybe you don't know all the facts."

"I'm aware of the facts."

"Your father wouldn't want to see his hotels go under, Laney. I'm sure he'd rather have you sell out than to have their reputation ruined. Your father was desperate to save them. That's why he called you home. He didn't know whom he could trust, other than you. He was under a great deal of stress. And now, you've admitted

that you're under that same sort of stress. He wouldn't want your health to suffer, Laney. And he wouldn't want you to go broke."

She gasped. "I'm not going broke, Evan. For heaven's sake."

The salad arrived along with a basket of assorted bread and Laney stopped speaking long enough to allow the waiter to place it on the table. Evan watched her pick up her fork and shuffle romaine spears around on her plate. Still, she didn't eat a bite.

"You will if your hotels don't stop draining your cash reserves."

Laney snapped her head up. "For all I know, you're the one behind the mishaps at Royal. You want them that badly."

Evan swore under his breath. "If you really believed that, you wouldn't be sitting here having dinner with me. No, I think you really want to hear what I have to say."

But they were once again interrupted when the waiter arrived. He set two plates of swordfish, garlic potatoes and creamed spinach before them. The mingling of aromas made his mouth water, but the arrival of the food had the opposite effect on Laney. She turned away from the sizzling hot plate.

"Is everything satisfactory?" the waiter asked.

"Yes, thank you," Evan answered. "That's all for now."

Laney picked up a forkful of greens and put them in her mouth. She chewed as if she were accomplishing a great feat. "I'm not sure what I believe about you, Evan.

But I need to know what happened that day between you and my father. And I'd appreciate the truth."

Laney didn't believe Evan Tyler. She sat back in the limousine after their dinner, rehashing his denials. Her traitorous stomach refused to calm. Her head swirled. She gazed out the window at the passing moonlit scenery as they drove home, so she wouldn't have to deal with Evan's close scrutiny.

It had been business as usual with Nolan Royal that day. Evan had said nothing out of the ordinary. He'd made his case, presented her father a fair deal and was willing to negotiate. He'd generously offered Nolan Royal a consulting position in the company once the deal was completed.

Laney could only imagine how that had gone over with her father. And even as Evan had spoken those well-rehearsed words to her, Laney knew he'd masked his contempt for her father. She'd done her homework and learned that Evan and his brothers had pursued the chain of Swan's Inns for a long time. They'd wined and dined Mr. Swan personally and spent a good deal of money trying to convince him to sell to Tempest. They wanted to expand, and the Inns would fit perfectly into their plans. But her father had an ace up his sleeve that no one had known about.

His tactics left something to be desired, yes. But Nolan Royal had come up from the ranks the hard way. He knew how to fight dirty if need be to save something

he treasured. He had something damaging on the proud, elderly Clayton Swan, something personal and something that might compromise his family life.

What Laney didn't know, was just how much coercion, if any, it had taken. It could have been simply that her father had made him a better deal all around. Laney wanted to think so. And that meant the Tempest Hotels lost out. And if there was one thing Laney had learned about Evan Tyler, it was he didn't like losing.

"I'm not giving up, Laney," Evan said as the driver pulled in to her driveway.

"I'm not selling, Evan." She couldn't betray her father's wishes. She'd made him a solemn promise. She'd work doubly hard to find out the cause of The Royals' problems, if need be. Preston had increased the security in the hotels and he'd persuaded her to hire a private investigator to get to the root of the trouble. Laney was sure that would help turn things around.

"Thank you for dinner. This concludes our business," she said rather stiffly. "Goodbye."

The limo driver opened the door and she feigned a smile at Evan Tyler before getting out.

It was best she didn't see him again until absolutely necessary. She didn't trust him. She wouldn't tell him about the baby. It was too much to deal with right now.

As soon as her feet hit the brick driveway, Laney's head spun in all directions. She straightened up, but that only made things worse. Her legs went weak and she fought dizziness. She tried blinking it away to gain

her equilibrium but when she turned toward her front door, she nearly keeled over.

"What the hell?" Evan was beside her instantly, casting her a concerned look. He grabbed her arm and guided her to the front door slowly. "Damn it, Laney. You should've eaten something back at the restaurant."

He took her purse and rummaged for her house keys, then opened her front door. Her mind fuzzy, she couldn't very well argue with him; she struggled just to keep upright. "I…can…manage…from here."

"Right," he said, lifting her up into both his arms and kicking the door open wide.

"I…didn't…invite…you…in." She stared into Evan's dark eyes for half a second, then her world went black.

It didn't take Evan long to find her master bedroom, the cottagelike home had airy open rooms. He carried her in and set her carefully onto a king-size bed. "Laney," he said, tapping her cheek. "Laney, wake up."

Her eyes fluttered opened. She stared at him. "What h-happened?"

"You fainted," he said. "You'll be fine in a second."

"I'm okay," she said, her eyes growing wide as she tried to lift up from the bed. "You don't have to stay."

He grabbed her shoulders and gently set her back down. "Stay put. You're in no shape to get up yet. I'll be right back."

Evan entered her master bath and grabbed a face

towel off the towel rack. He rinsed it under the faucet with cold water and squeezed out the excess. As he turned off the faucet and exited the bathroom, something he'd glimpsed struck him as odd. Quickly, he retraced his steps and glanced down into the wastebasket beside the marble sink.

The box lay at the bottom of the trash, its initials angled up toward him, leaving no room for doubt.

e.p.t.

A home pregnancy test.

Evan stared at the box a good long moment.

And then it all made sense.

Laney was pregnant.

The last few times he'd seen her, she'd appeared pale, sort of washed out, so unlike the healthy tanned Laney he'd known in Hawaii. He'd known her body intimately and noticed she'd lost some weight, as well. Hadn't he heard the account of his own mother's pregnancy enough times to recognize it when the symptoms stared him right smack in the face?

How could he have missed those signs?

Laney passed it off as stress. He'd known it was something more. But he wouldn't have guessed it was that much *more*. A child. Evan could hardly believe it. If she hadn't fainted, he might not have found out. Damn it. He had a right to know. When the hell did she plan on telling him?

Anger boiled just below the surface.

Laney's eyes were closed when he entered her

bedroom again and sat on the bed. He set the cool moistened towel across her forehead.

"Thank you," she said quietly. "That feels good."

Evan noted the serene look on her face, then he glanced around the room filled with girlie things, lace and frills and walls tinted with deep rose-colored shades. On those rose-colored walls, were framed photographs, black and whites, color prints and sepias. She'd surrounded herself with what she loved. Her photographs told her story better than anything else. Her father hadn't recognized her talent. He hadn't known the true Elena Royal.

He stared at the one photo he recognized, a view of the Pacific from atop the Haleakala Crater and memories flooded in, banking his rising fury. "When were you going to tell me?"

"Tell you *what?*"

He sucked in a breath. "About the baby."

Her eyes popped open. Reflexively, her hand braced her abdomen. That gesture spelled it out better than a dozen pregnancy tests.

With a panicked look on her face, she tried getting up again, but he blocked her and shook his head. "You are pregnant, aren't you, Laney?"

Fear, regret and defeat all registered on her face. She laid her head on the pillow, then nodded.

"How…pregnant?" he asked tersely.

Laney had to know what he was asking. Was he the father? After all, she'd been engaged and ready to be married right before he'd met her.

"Seven weeks."

He did the math. She'd been with him exactly seven weeks ago on that island.

"Are you sure?"

"The doctor confirmed it."

"When? How long have you known?"

"I saw him yesterday morning."

Evan's jaw clenched. He ran his hands through his hair and sucked in oxygen, then bolted from the bed and paced back and forth to release excess energy. Adrenaline pumped through his veins like raging wildfire. "You've seen me twice since then and didn't tell me?"

Laney sat upright on the bed and rubbed her head. "I was trying to adjust to the idea."

"Damn it. It's not an idea. It's a baby."

She remained seated, probably fearful of rising and fainting again. That was just fine with him. He needed to hash this out with her. Fainting wasn't an option.

"I meant you, Evan. I needed to adjust to you being the father."

Evan let go a string of curses.

Laney stood. He watched her legs wobble a little, but she held her ground. He was red-hot and ticked off. Yet, at the same time concerned for the baby.

His baby.

"Sit down, Laney. Let's talk about this."

"I'm not ready to talk about it."

"Sit." He pointed to the bed. "I'll do all the talking."

"Imagine that," she muttered, but she sat anyway.

"I'm marrying you. As soon as I can make the arrangements, we'll have a small ceremony and—"

"Whoa!" Laney put up a stopping hand. "Are you crazy? I will not marry you."

Evan scoffed at her refusal. "It's not negotiable."

"It's not negotiable?" A hot gleam of anger crossed her features. "Okay, I lied. It's *not* your baby. It's Joe the bartender's. Remember him?"

Evan braced his hands on his hips. "Sure do. Good old *married* Joe. His wife, Tessie, waited tables at the Wind Breeze and never let him out of her sight. Nice try."

Laney rolled her eyes.

"Don't deny it, Laney. The baby is mine." Evan was sure of it now. If it weren't she wouldn't have had such a panicked look on her face when he discovered the truth. At least, she'd been honest about the time frame. They'd spent a lot of time in and out of bed those days. Evan would bank his last dollar that she hadn't been with another man while on the island. She wouldn't have admitted to him that he was the father otherwise. After all, he knew she thought of him as the enemy, the man responsible for all of her current problems. "And you will marry me."

Laney frowned, her eyes narrowing. "You'd do anything to get your hands on The Royals, wouldn't you?"

"If you remember, *your* hands were on me—all over me, babe, at least half a dozen times. So don't go pointing fingers. We're both responsible for this."

"I'm willing to take *full* responsibility." She cast him a dry look. "You're off the hook."

"Hell would have to freeze over first. And you know damn well this isn't about the hotels, Laney. You're carrying my child. My flesh and blood. I'm giving that child a name. And making damn sure you take care of yourself while you carry him to term."

"Don't even suggest I'm not taking care of this child!"

"Prove it. Marry me."

"My answer is no." She folded her arms across her middle, shook her head and stared at him.

He stared back. If she wanted a contest of wills, she'd get one. "Let me put it this way. My child will have my name and my protection. If you don't accept this proposal, I can guarantee your hotels will fail and it won't be pretty, Laney. You're out of your depth with this. I've rescued failing enterprises and brought new life into them. That's how Tempest has thrived against worthy competitors. Now, do you or don't you want to save The Royals?"

Six

Two weeks later, Laney stood with one hand holding a bouquet of white fragrant gardenias, while the other hand clasped onto Julia like a sinking swimmer clutching at a lifeguard. "I can't believe I married him."

Julia hugged her close, whispering in her ear as they stood in the vestibule of the Beverly Hills Courthouse, "You're doing it for the baby, honey. You're giving him legitimacy and saving your father's company all at one time."

Though unconvinced, Laney nodded as she peered across the hallway, watching Evan shake hands with his brother Trent. He'd flown in from Texas for the wedding and was leaving later tonight. Evan and Laney had agreed on having one person stand up for each of them

during the civil ceremony and Trent had been the brother to win the coin flip. Laney's decision had been much easier. She couldn't imagine this day without Julia by her side.

"But maybe the price is too high."

"Laney, look at him. He's not exactly your average Joe. He's a good-looking devil, intelligent and focused and I have a feeling that this might work out for you."

"*Devil* being the key word here."

Julia shook her head solemnly. "I don't know. He promised to help The Royals out of financial ruin. And he accepted your terms for the prenuptial agreement. You retain full ownership of The Royals. He has nothing else to gain. If you let me play the advocate for a second, I think all he really wants is a place in his child's life. Besides," Julia said almost wistfully, "he's got a gorgeous brother."

Laney looked at Trent and let go a quiet chuckle. "If you like the tall, dark and incredibly rugged type." She'd been introduced to Trent right before the short ceremony.

"What's not to like about a man who can pull off wearing a Stetson in the heart of L.A.?"

But Laney thought Evan the better looking of the two. He wore a stylish three-piece black suit, white shirt and gray silk tie, appearing dashing and handsome and…smug.

Darn him.

She'd resisted his daily proposals and had actually gotten good at saying no to him, though he'd been

doggedly persistent, claiming he wouldn't give up. He wouldn't allow her to shove him out of the baby's life.

To add to that, there had been another costly problem at Royal since she found out about the baby. Laney and her team had done everything in their power to figure out a solution, but with having queasy days, Evan showing up on her doorstep every night and mountains of additional paperwork piling up, Laney knew she couldn't do it all alone anymore.

She'd given it a good deal of thought and had finally concluded that raising a child without his father wasn't right. She couldn't quite bring herself to deny her child a family life, even if it were in name only.

Somehow Evan managed to convince her marrying him would solve her problems. She had to honor the vow she'd made to her father. She wanted to save The Royals.

Evan had pulled out all the stops, including showing her his portfolio, his track record with hotel management and his profit-and-loss statements.

Laney knew he was a sound businessman.

But she didn't think she'd wind up married to him.

She swallowed hard. Her stomach was nervous again, but this time it was less a baby disruption and more a my-God-what-have-I-done disruption.

In the back of her mind, she couldn't help but wonder if Evan was behind the problems Royal was having. Was he guilty of sabotaging the company? Had she married the enemy?

Having his baby complicated her life on so many

levels. How could she ever trust Evan Tyler, the man she'd spoken vows with today?

As they exited the courthouse, Evan held firmly on to her arm. "Be prepared and smile," he said with a note of caution and before she could sort through his confusing statement they were caught up in a whirlwind of photographers and news reporters. News vans from four different television stations converged on the street. Photos were snapped and reporters rushed up to them. Evan shielded Laney from the brunt of the madness, and soon Trent and Julia came up to stand beside them as the reporters unleashed a flurry of questions.

"What does this marriage mean to Tempest Hotels?"

"Would you classify this marriage as a business merger?"

"How did you and Elena Royal meet?"

"Mrs. Tyler, only a few months ago you were engaged to someone else. Why the rushed marriage?"

"My wife will not comment," Evan said. "I'll answer your questions for both of us. Laney and I met some time ago. Her engagement to Overton was a mistake. We've decided to marry now because…" He then stopped to take her hand in his and peer into her eyes.

Laney squeezed his hand as hard as she could while retaining her composure. Good God, he wasn't going to tell the world she was pregnant, was he? She might as well murder him now and get it over with.

"…we can't live without each other. I think that says

it all. Now, as far as the hotels go, my wife will retain full ownership of The Royals, but I'll be at the helm right along with her. I plan to take an active role with The Royals although Tempest and The Royals will operate separately. Our marriage is the only merger today—" Evan winked at Laney "—I'm happy to say."

One pushy reporter called out, "Why the secret, civil ceremony?"

"One, it's not a secret. My office alerted all of you about the ceremony. And two, my wife's father just passed away. We didn't want to dishonor his memory with a lavish wedding at this time. Certainly, Nolan Royal deserves that much respect."

Evan answered a few more questions with wit and charm, protecting her from the onslaught. Laney watched him work the crowd of reporters. He controlled the situation with poised finesse. Finally he said, "I think you've got it all. Now, if you'll excuse us, we have to get on with our honeymoon."

"Where's the honeymoon?" several reporters asked simultaneously.

"No comment on that one." Evan grinned as he led Laney toward the limo.

Once they were seated, along with Julia and Trent, and the driver pulled away from the courthouse, Laney turned to Evan, her nerves raw. The last thing she expected was to find a dozen reporters outside the courthouse on her wedding day. "You called those news stations. You knew they'd show up here. Why on earth did you do that?"

Evan rested a hand on her knee and smiled, first looking at Trent, then to her. "First rule of business, babe. Send your message loud and clear."

"What message?"

He rubbed his hand along her upper leg and made mush of her thought process. She wore an ivory two-piece suit with a tailored jacket and knee-length skirt, simple and tasteful for their civil ceremony wedding and now he was taking full advantage of that exposed knee.

"If they mess with Royal or you, then they have to answer to me."

Trent leaned back in the seat facing her, stretching out his long legs. "Ev's got a reputation in the business for being—"

"Ruthless?" Laney interrupted, then gasped when she realized how awful that might have sounded to Evan's brother. "I'm sorry. I shouldn't have said that."

"Apology accepted," Evan said immediately, casting her a somber look and lacing his fingers with hers.

Darn him. The apology was meant for Trent, but leave it to Evan to twist her intentions around. He set his hand over her knee again, now entwined in her fingers. Laney couldn't very well shove his hand off her without garnering attention from Julia and Trent.

Trent grinned. "You two are a match made in heaven, I see. I was going to say, Ev's got a reputation for being steadfast and tenacious. He's not a man to double-cross."

Laney understood that. And that's exactly why she

couldn't believe that he hadn't created trouble in her father's office the day he died. And she was appalled at his high-handed tactics today. At the very least, he could have warned her ahead of time about the news reporters outside. The last thing Laney Royal needed was undue negative attention. She'd gone out of her way to avoid it after her engagement fiasco with Justin Overton. And today, Evan had purposely invited the press into their lives.

Laney secretly fumed, but she'd save her wrath for when she was alone with Evan.

Trent raised a flute of champagne. "To my brother, Evan, his beautiful new wife, Laney, and to the little baby who'll call me Uncle Trent soon. Congratulations."

Julia raised her flute of champagne, as well, while Evan and Laney lifted the glasses of sparkling cider Evan had ordered for both of them.

They toasted then sipped their drinks. Awkward silence followed as they sat at a private table for four in a cozy elegant restaurant on Santa Monica Boulevard. Trent insisted they celebrate in style and Laney didn't have the heart to refuse the kind offer.

Trent broke the stifling quiet when he questioned Julia. "How long have you two been friends?"

Julia smiled when she looked at her and Laney's nerves calmed. Her friend had that effect on her and right now she appreciated the comfort. "Since babyhood, right, Laney?"

"Yes, our mothers had been close friends."

Julia laughed. "We really had no choice in the matter. It's a good thing we liked each other while growing up."

Laney was aware of Evan watching her. Every time she glanced his way, his eyes were on her. While Julia sat beside her on one side, calming her, Evan sat on the other having the opposite effect. She hadn't forgotten the sizzling hot nights she'd spent with him at the Wind Breeze. She'd been wildly attracted to him and he'd been the balm she'd needed to heal her broken heart. When he'd walked out of her hotel room that last day, she thought she'd seen the last of him. Now here she was, married to him and carrying his child.

If only she could look at him and not doubt his intentions. If only she could allow herself the freedom to let down her guard. But she'd learned her lesson with both Justin and Evan and she wouldn't be fooled again.

Laney sat quietly for most of the dinner, listening to Trent and Julia make small talk while she ignored her husband. She was fully aware that he noticed every small bite she managed to take during the meal. She'd ordered filet mignon with all the trimmings and thanks to the nausea pills she decided to take, eating a small meal wasn't so much of a chore anymore. When she pushed her plate away, Evan assessed the remainder of her meal and appeared relieved that she'd eaten half her food.

Trent had ordered a wedding cake that the baker de-

livered personally to the table along with his good wishes. Laney even managed to down half a slice. But then her stomach rebelled and she put her hand to her flat belly.

"What's wrong?" Evan asked, not missing a thing.

"Nothing really. Same old, same old," she said, trying for humor.

Julia added her concern. "You do look a little tired, honey."

Laney attempted to console her friend. "I'm fine, Jules. It's been a long day."

Evan nodded, setting his napkin on the table. "It's time we headed home." He glanced at Trent and Julia. "Please stay and finish your cake and coffee. And thank you both. Trent, I'm glad you stood up for me today. I'll be sure to do the same for you one day."

Trent's amused look told them all what he thought of that idea. He shook Evan's hand. "Congratulations, Ev." Then he leaned over and kissed her cheek. "And Laney, welcome to the family. Go easy on Evan. He's in enough trouble right now. Our mother's going to hang his hide for not telling her about the wedding."

Evan twisted his mouth, but true regret entered his eyes belying his next words. "I'll handle Mom when she gets back from her cruise."

"Sure you will," Trent said, keeping his tone light. "Don't worry about us. I'll take Julia home, if that's okay with you?" Trent looked at Julia.

Julia nodded. "Thank you. I appreciate that."

And after Laney and Julia embraced and said good-bye, Evan escorted her out of the restaurant.

To begin married life together.

Laney glanced down at the four-carat flawless pear-shaped diamond ring Evan had placed on her finger during the civil ceremony. The thoughtful gesture surprised her even though she could hardly believe she was married now and looking around Evan's spacious penthouse apartment at the top of the Tempest tower.

There was a progressive feel to the surroundings with dark lacquered furniture against pristine white walls. The artwork modern, the rooms seemingly stark but for the tasteful pieces of necessary furniture. No fluff here.

The contrast between The Royals and Tempest hotels lay in the decor. Where The Royals were known for warmth in color, draperies, carpeting and good old-fashioned charm, Tempest was known for smooth sleek furniture, contemporary styling and airy rooms. The two hotel chains were as different as night and day. Much like Laney and her new husband, she thought solemnly.

Evan placed a hand at her back and guided her farther into the living room. "This will only be temporary. The baby will need a backyard."

"My Brentwood home has a yard."

Evan shook his head. "It's too small for a family, Laney. We'll need more room."

Family? Laney trembled inside. Did he expect them to behave as a family with strolls in the park and Sunday picnics and happily ever after?

Did he expect them to have more children?

Laney married Evan so that her child would have a legitimate name and two parents who loved him or her. She married Evan so that he could stop the damage to The Royals. She married him, to honor her vow to her father. Yet, she wasn't even sure the marriage would last past the first year. Evan clearly only married her because of the baby. And she could say the same.

"We'll move as soon as possible," Evan added, pouring himself a whiskey from the bar.

"If we do, it'll be by mutual consent. I don't like surprises, Evan. Just don't pull another stunt like you did with the news reporters today. You could have informed me about your plans."

"And you would have said...?"

"That I'd rather not have my picture splashed all over the six o'clock news."

"I told you my reasons for that." Evan sipped his drink, watching her carefully over the edge of his tumbler.

"I'm half of this partnership. Don't ever forget that."

He set his glass down and approached her, his eyes gleaming with heat. "Just so we're clear, this is not a business partnership. The prenup took care of that. This is a marriage. You're my wife now."

"You blackmailed me into this marriage."

Evan shook his head. "I only spelled out the truth."

"You offered to save The Royals. And I accepted. You knew how desperate I was."

"I go after what I want, babe," he said, standing close, studying her face. "That's not a bad thing." His voice was husky and low. He unfastened all three buttons on her blazer. The jacket front opened to expose the matching ivory shell underneath. Evan circled his hands around her bringing her closer, his fingers spreading up to nudge the base of her breasts.

"What are you doing?" she whispered, her nipples growing taut from the slight caress.

"Kissing my new wife." He bent his head and lowered his mouth to take her in a deep, slow, leisurely kiss. He tasted of whiskey and power and confidence. Laney fell into the kiss, his lips expertly blending with hers, making her remember things she'd done with him that she'd wanted so badly to forget.

He caressed her nipples, grazing his thumbs over her lazily, creating sharp electric shocks that rushed through her body.

When he broke the kiss and looked into her eyes, Laney's mind spun for a moment. How easy it would be to forget who he was, and how he'd used and manipulated her. How easy it would be to fall victim to his dark piercing eyes, handsome face and gorgeous body.

But Laney wouldn't forget. She backed out of his arms. "I'm tired and need to rest. Will you show me to my room?"

Evan drew breath into his lungs and she took great satisfaction seeing him appear disappointed.

"I put your things in the master bedroom."

She followed him down a hallway. He stopped to lean against the doorjamb to a huge room with a glorious view. "This is it."

She strolled past him and into the room, taking it all in quickly. "Thanks. This is…nice." Though she wished she could sleep in her own bed tonight with all her familiar comforts, she had to face the fact that she was a married woman now. She was expected to live with her husband.

Evan wouldn't have it any other way. She'd tried to convince him she'd be better off living at her own place without him, but she'd known that was one argument she wouldn't win.

Her life had taken a drastic turn over the last few months. Adjusting wouldn't be easy. The only thing she clung to with any joy in her heart was the baby she nurtured. She turned to him. "Where will you be sleeping?"

Evan pulled away from the doorjamb and laughed as though genuinely amused. "Get some rest, Laney." He turned and once he walked out of her line of vision, she closed the door.

Evan chucked his suit jacket and vest then unfastened his tie, tossing them onto a lounge chair on the balcony. He paced back and forth as he spoke to his brother Brock

on the speakerphone. Starlight twinkled above; the city below still hummed with late-night traffic. "Yes, that's right. Get in touch with Landon. We need someone to dig real deep into The Royals' infrastructure."

"Landon's security team is the best. Pricey, bro. And in demand."

"Brock, I don't want his team. I want Landon to personally oversee this. Offer your friend whatever it takes. Call in a favor if you have to."

Brock whistled low and long. "You're serious about this, aren't you?"

"When have you known me not to be serious about business?"

"Yeah, speaking about that, what the hell are you doing on the phone with me? Didn't you marry a pretty blonde today? Isn't this your wedding night? Or is the honeymoon over already?"

It wasn't the sultry summer air making him sweat, but the reminder of Laney sleeping in his bed, that had him unbuttoning his shirt and rolling up his sleeves. "You let me worry about my honeymoon, Brock. Just be sure to get in touch with Landon. Tell him my concerns about The Royals and then have him call me tomorrow. I want to roll with this as soon as possible."

Brock hesitated. "Got it. And, hey, I didn't mean to yank your chain."

Evan picked up his drink and sipped whiskey. "You didn't. Laney's not feeling well. She's resting right now."

"Still can't stand the sight of you?"

There was no mirth in Brock's question and Evan knew it wasn't a playful taunt. This time Brock had spoken with sincerity.

"I'm sure this marriage wasn't in her plans. It wasn't in mine, either."

"And neither was fatherhood."

"No, but you and I both know what it was like growing up without our father." Evan shoved overwhelming guilt from his mind. He had enough to think about right now. "There's no way my child is coming into this world without me by his side. And I plan on being there all through his life. Laney is just going to have to accept that."

After he and Brock finalized their plans, his brother added one more thing. "Congratulations, Ev. On your marriage and the baby. I hope it works out for you."

"It will," Evan said resolutely. He wasn't one to surrender to defeat. "And, thanks."

After he hung up with Brock, Evan stared out into the warm summer night sky. He finished his drink thinking of Laney and how she must look, sprawled out on his bedsheets right now, her blond hair spilling onto his pillow.

"What the hell," he said, setting his tumbler down. He left the balcony, entered the apartment and stripped down to his boxers. When he walked into his bedroom, all was quiet. Laney looked better than he imagined wearing a blue silk nightie, her body curving deliciously on the bed, her slender legs, half in and half out of the sheets.

Evan strolled to his side of the bed and lay down

carefully, making sure not to wake her. When he rolled over to face her back and breathe in the lingering scent of gardenia she'd had in her hair earlier, she stirred.

"What are you doing?" she whispered.

He smiled. So she wasn't asleep. "You keep asking me that."

"I don't want to sleep with you."

He kept his voice low. "Yes, you do. But not tonight, babe." He kissed the back of her neck then began massaging her shoulders. "Just relax. You're too tense. I thought you'd be asleep by now."

"Hard to relax after the day I've had," she said, her voice more mellow now.

"You mean after marrying the enemy?"

Evan continued to rub her shoulders, spurred on by her little purring moans. He banked his own rising desire, his palms itching to touch more of her, his body aching for satisfaction, but Laney needed rest tonight. She needed to find comfort in his bed and to accept her fate.

"Yes," she replied, her voice fading, "married to the…enemy."

Only when he heard the soft sounds of her slumber did Evan take his hands from her shoulders, allowing her the sleep she needed.

He had never slept with a woman without *sleeping* with her. She was his wife, legally bound to him, and he had to leave her untouched on their wedding night.

The irony didn't escape him.

But it sure as hell irritated him.

Seven

Laney opened her eyes to unfamiliar surroundings. The massive bed she found herself in nearly swallowed her whole. She untangled herself from the sheets and lifted up, rubbing her head. Through her sleep-hazy mind, the events of the past twenty-four hours flashed.

She was in Evan Tyler's bed. In the Tempest Hotel. She'd married him.

Oh, God.

"Did you sleep well?"

Laney turned her head toward the large floor-to-ceiling window overlooking the Beverly Center. Evan stood with his back to her, sipping coffee as he peered out to the dawning day.

Laney admired his physical form, the navy boxers he

wore clung to his perfect rear end. Rippled with muscle across broad shoulders, his skin glistened against the backdrop of stark walls. She remembered how he'd once felt under her palms, her hands skimming over that lean strong back and riding down farther to glide over a firm tight butt.

For a second she allowed herself the clear memory of making love to him in Maui. Then she put her head down again and massaged her temples. "I, uh, slept pretty well, actually."

The nausea pills were working. She hoped she'd seen the last of those spells.

Evan turned around, his eyes meeting hers. Sleep tousled, with his hair mussed and a shadow of a beard, he took her breath away. Raw, unwelcome heat surged straight through her. She couldn't deny her attraction to him. They had heat and chemistry. But she couldn't forget who he was.

"Breakfast is outside on the balcony."

Laney nodded, then ran her fingers through her hair. She'd spent her wedding night with a man she would never have married. A man she didn't trust. A man who'd probably never slept beside a woman without having mind-blowing sex with her during the night. And now, they were trying to pretend everything was normal. "This is awkward."

"It's not exactly a Disney adventure for me, either, babe."

She bounded off the bed, dragging the sheet over her

to cover her nightgown. For some odd reason, his comment injured her pride. "This wasn't *my* idea. I could always go home."

Evan placed his coffee cup down and approached her. "You still don't get it, Laney. You *are* home."

"It'll never feel like home to me."

Evan gripped the sheet and pulled it slowly from her hands, exposing her, both body and soul.

Hunger gleamed in his eyes. His face unmasked, jolting, penetrating desire crossed his features. "It was a hell of a wedding night."

Laney trembled. She feared his desire would ignite her own. She took a quick breath. "It's how it has to be from now on."

Evan reached out to touch her shoulders and bring her closer. "I can't accept that."

She shook her head. "You have to, it's for the—"

He covered her mouth with his, taking her in a hard, crushing kiss, his overwhelming passion sweeping her up and carrying her away. She returned the kiss freely, seduced by his expert mouth, the heat of his body and the memory of wild island nights.

Her rational mind battled for control. She put her hands on his bare chest to shove him away, but she couldn't quite manage it. He felt too good under her palms. The small force she summoned up was immediately forgotten when he parted her lips and mated their tongues. She melted into his kiss and moaned with pleasure. "Ty."

She gasped and broke off the kiss, stunned by where her mind had gone.

He cupped her head in both hands and looked into her eyes. "We had something back there on the island," he whispered. "I didn't forget."

"It was a lie. You're a liar."

"I lied, yes. But I'm not sorry."

He hooked his fingers under the spaghetti straps of her nightgown and slid them down her arms. The material barely clung on, teasing the tips of her nipples. "I'm your husband now, babe. Be *bold*. Trust me."

He bunched up the material of her nightgown at the hem and lowered it down with a quick move until she was fully exposed. She refused to flinch or show any embarrassment. "I am bold. I married you. But I'll never trust you."

He swept his gaze over her body then took a sharp breath. "We'll work on that. *Later.*"

Then he kissed her again with urgency and unshielded passion that Laney wasn't strong enough to refuse. When he lowered her onto the bed, she went willingly.

At that very moment, she found her new husband infuriatingly irresistible.

Minutes later, Evan brought her to the brink of satisfaction, his skilled hands and perfect mouth exploring her body with slow and deliberate moves. He cupped her head, kissed her lips and slid his hands all over, tempting and teasing her until "ooohs" of pleasure and wrung-out pleas for more escaped her throat.

His silken erection rubbed her belly then nudged the moist tip of her womanhood. Laney parted her legs and welcomed him, her body a betrayer of her heart, yet the sense of fulfillment she experienced when he thrust inside, stunned her.

"Ah, Laney," he said, his head down, allowing them both time to absorb the earth-shattering effect of the connection. "You feel so damn good."

Heart racing and body shaking, Laney wouldn't utter those words back to him. But she felt the same way. Physically, Evan Tyler was all a woman could want in a man.

He didn't allow her time to dwell on those thoughts. He moved inside her, filling her, thrusting slowly, taking his time and she joined him, their bodies undulating and fully in sync with one another.

The slow easy rhythm they created compared to the sexy sounds of smooth jazz they'd heard at Good Sax. Laney dipped and rose and swayed, imagining the saxophone playing as she followed Evan's fluid moves. He bent to kiss her lips, then lowered his mouth to place reverent kisses on her breasts. There was a difference in his lovemaking now, the desperate wildness was gone, replaced by a pace that spoke of many days and nights to come.

Laney squeezed her eyes shut at the thought. She married the enemy. She'd have to deal with the guilt, but now she only relished the heady sensations Evan created. His thrusts deepened, his body grew tight, filling her. He braced his arms around her lifting her up. She wrapped her legs around his waist and watched the

sheer force and power on his face as he held back to allow her a complete and potent climax.

"Let it go, babe," he whispered with encouragement.

Trembling, Laney couldn't hold back her release. The measured bursts spiraled down and a sense of completion took hold like a tightly coiled snake finally unwinding, allowing her short gasping breaths of air.

Evan's thrusts deepened, bringing her with him again. She knew the moment he let go, relinquishing his power and strength for just those few unguarded moments. Intense pleasure registered on his face, a raw need that elicited a groan of satisfaction.

For a moment, Laney savored the fact that she brought him such enjoyment. But when he rolled off her and sprawled beside her, resting on his back to stare at the ceiling, she admonished herself for the part she'd played in that.

Her body sated, Laney drew air deep into her lungs, refueling her resolve. Guilt ate at her. Evan might have been responsible for her father's death. He tricked her and manipulated her and resorted to sugarcoated blackmail to marry her. She pressed her lips together. They still tasted of him. Confused and hormonal, tears filled her eyes.

Evan rolled over to her, placing a gentle hand atop her stomach where their baby grew inside. "You're my wife now, in every respect."

Laney's eyes went wide with realization. "You bastard," she hissed, immediate anger driving her from the bed. She rose up quickly, threw on her nightgown and

looked at him, her face burning with fury. "All you care about is sealing the deal. Getting the job done. I'm nothing more to you than a transaction! You have no soul, Evan Tyler."

Evan bounded up from the bed, his eyes hot, his face flaming from her accusations. He stood naked in all his glory, shaking his head. "What the hell are you talking about, Laney?"

She pointed her finger. "You…you're only interested in the bottom line, Evan. And unfortunately, that means me this time. I'm your bottom line."

He shook his head again. "Laney, damn it. Calm down. We just made love on that bed two minutes ago." He pointed to the rumpled sheets. "And now I have no idea what you're talking about."

"I'm talking about your trap! You only wanted to consummate the marriage. Another way to insure your place in my child's life. Don't deny it, Evan! Because I know better now."

He sent up a dozen vivid curses toward the ceiling then faced her, his eyes dark and dangerous. "Damn right I wanted to consummate the marriage. When are you going to get it through your head? We're married. You. And me. That means sleeping with your husband."

Laney fumed, her body boiling with rage. "With any other man, I'd believe that. But not with you. I'll never believe you. You might conquer my body, Evan. But you'll never own my heart. *Never.*"

"Laney, I never said I wanted your heart."

Laney's pulse escalated, but her stomach plummeted, his remark hitting her harder than she would have imagined. "No, you only wanted my hotels."

He looked her square in the eyes and spoke quietly. "I want our baby to come into this world with two parents who'll love him. Now just relax. Have some breakfast. I'm getting dressed and going into the office."

"Fine." She closed her eyes briefly. "Just go."

Laney folded her arms across her middle and stared out the window until she heard Evan shower, dress and leave.

She made her way to the balcony where a table was set for two and a lavish breakfast awaited her. She tried to ignore the dozen fragrant gardenias floating in a water vase that centered the table. Evan's doing no doubt, but she couldn't credit him with the thoughtful gesture. He didn't deserve her gratitude.

She sat, drew a deep breath and calmed herself. The baby needed nourishment and she needed to bolster her energy. Nothing was more important to her than having a healthy pregnancy.

Soon summer sunlight enveloped the shady balcony and Laney finished her meal quickly, opting for fresh melons and berries and eggs Benedict. Then she showered and dressed and drove to The Royals office.

She had a hotel empire to run.

By ten o'clock in the morning everyone in her office staff came by offering curious and cautious congratulations.

It seemed her marriage had been the highlight of the late-night news and the hot topic of gossip at The Royals' watercooler. Laney offered no excuses, gave no explanations. In little more than a month her reasons would become abundantly clear. Laney rested her hand on her abdomen, a protective gesture to the innocent baby that would become the very center of her life soon. And her only real family. Laney didn't want trouble of any kind to touch this child, though making that happen when she was in constant conflict with the baby's father, would be easier said than done.

She looked up from her desk when Preston walked in wearing a scowl on his handsome face. "Elena, I can't believe it." He crossed the space between them quickly and braced his hands on the desk, leaning toward her, his blue eyes dark with accusation. "You *married* him." He shook his head and asked in utter disbelief, "Why?"

Remorse set in. Preston had been her rock lately. She relied on him to guide her, lend her support and keep her sane when her father died. She couldn't blame him for feeling betrayed. "I had my reasons, Preston."

"Are you forgetting he was the last person to see your father alive? Who knows what he said to aggravate Nolan straight into heart failure?"

Ally walked in, carrying a tray. "Excuse me," she said, after a brisk knock. "I made you herbal tea." She hesitated at the door. "And Chef Merino sent in your favorite cranberry and nut scones with Devonshire cream."

Grateful for the interruption, Laney waved her secretary in. Laney didn't want to think about Preston's stinging accusations about Evan Tyler. In truth, she'd had all the same doubts about the man she married. But, she'd done what she needed to do for the sake of her child and her father's legacy. "Ally, thank you. It's just what I need right now."

Her father's secretary and personal aide had been looking after her since his death, too. Ally had been a godsend on the emotional front, offering tremendous strength to Laney during the hard times.

"I'll just leave the tray here and let you get back—"

"No, please stay," Laney said. "Both of you, sit down. I want to speak to you."

Ally set the tray of tea and scones on a side table, glanced at Preston, who looked none too pleased, and both took a seat in the chairs facing her desk.

"I know you both must be confused and completely thrown by...by my marriage," she began, closing her eyes briefly, wrestling with just the right words to say. "But I can assure you, I haven't gone off the deep end."

Preston pressed his lips tight. "Elena, what else can we think? What possible reason would you have to marry Evan Tyler? Do I have to remind you he's been after this company for a long time?"

"I'm going to help my wife get her company back."

The sound of Evan's commanding voice snapped her head up. He strode into the office and came to stand behind the desk, next to her, surprising everyone in the room.

"W-What are you doing here?" Laney asked, glancing up at him.

Evan smiled at Laney then set his eyes on the two coworkers wearing stunned expressions. "I'm dividing my time between Tempest and The Royals now." He set his hand on Laney's shoulder and looked into her eyes. "We need to get The Royals operating smoothly before we can take a honeymoon, right, babe?"

Laney glanced at papers on her desk, trying to calm the angry tirade ready to build. She'd hoped she wouldn't see Evan until tonight. She still smarted from his tactics this morning. But she'd come to the conclusion that she was just as much to blame. She had to be more wary of her new husband. He was an expert manipulator and he certainly knew how to work his way around a bedroom. "Yes, uh, right."

Preston stood. "Elena, what's going on here?"

"What's going on here," Evan replied, bracing his hands on the desk and leaning forward to address his wife's right-hand man, "is that Laney and I will work as a team from now on. Ally, I've got a desk being delivered today. Please see that it's placed right next to my wife's."

Laney glanced at him and whispered, "You're moving into my office?"

"It's the best way, don't you agree, sweetheart?"

Preston flinched.

Ally smiled.

Laney stood and peered into his eyes. "I'd like a

word with my…husband, please. Alone." She looked at Preston and Ally. "We'll finish this conversation later."

"Of course," Ally said, then she glanced at Evan. "Congratulations."

Preston added his own congratulations, shaking Evan's hand before exiting the office. Evan admired his restraint. Clearly Preston Malloy didn't like Evan's presence at Royal one bit. He hated that he'd married Laney. Evan had seen jealousy before in men, but Malloy appeared equally frustrated and protective, as well.

Evan figured he'd come up against his share of wary employees in the coming weeks. He'd win them over as soon as the company started making money again.

He grabbed a scone and took a bite.

Laney stood, her pretty blue eyes lit with fire. "Don't ever strong-arm me that way in front of my employees again, Evan."

"I was just stating my case."

"You mean staking your claim."

Evan loved Laney's wit. She was quick and sharp. She had more of her old man in her than she might think. Nolan Royal had been a force to be reckoned with, until old age had worn him down and heartbreak over his wife's death had softened him.

"That, too. I want people to know who they're dealing with. From now on, nothing gets to you without going by me first."

She narrowed her eyes. And looked so damn enticing in the pin-striped business suit that hugged all her

curves. The harder she tried not to look sexy, the more his imagination took flight. The tailored white blouse dipping low and forming a V underneath reminded him of where his lips had been this morning.

"You have no legal right to be here, you know."

Evan threw his head back and laughed. "Tossing that prenup in my face already? I thought it might take longer than twenty-four hours for that. I'm aware of all the reasons you married me."

Then he bent his head to lay a long lazy kiss on her. Her quick intake of breath turned him on even more. His teeth tugged gently on her lips, drawing them out so he could stroke his tongue over her mouth. She offered up a tiny pleasured sound.

She wanted him, physically. She couldn't hide that fact. Not after the mind-blowing sex they'd had this morning, but she'd laid down a challenge.

And he'd lied.

Laney, I never said I wanted your heart.

Evan Tyler was an all or nothing kind of man. He wanted Laney, *all* of her and he'd take up her challenge and do his best to change her mind. She was his wife and he didn't take marriage lightly. They had a responsibility to their baby and to themselves.

No way would Laney Tyler, his new wife, put him off in or out of the bedroom.

Eight

"I thought these attacks on the hotels would stop once I married you," Laney said a week later, going over the reports on her desk.

Evan glanced at her from his side of the office, his eyes narrowing. "I work fast, but not that fast, babe. I've got the best man in the business investigating."

"And I told you, we have our own investigator."

"Nobody is like Code Landon. He's got a sixth sense about these things."

"Code?" Laney shook her head. "You've got to be kidding. Sounds like he's right out of a secret agent comic book."

Evan grinned. "Trust me. Cody Nash Landon is no

comic book character. Though he gets the job done, every time." Then he added, "We have that in common."

Laney twisted her lips. She had to admit, her husband had taken the reins at Royal and she'd already seen a difference in the way the hotels operated. Together, they'd worked side by side for the past week and after she'd gotten over her initial resentment of him being at the helm alongside her, she could honestly say they worked well together.

She still didn't trust him. She kept feeling that soon, he'd pull the rug out from under her. But for the time being, they were managing pretty well.

"So tell me, which of my competitors would stand to gain the most from our hotels faltering?"

Evan shook his head. He stood to glance out the window briefly, then he faced her, his expression sober. "What if I told you The Royals are being sabotaged from within? What if I told you someone on the inside is doing this?"

Laney rose, her heart racing, her mind spinning. "You can't mean that, Evan."

He took steps to come face-to-face with her. "Not only do I mean it, I'm sure of it."

"I don't believe you. My father prided himself on his staff. Loyalty to the company was always foremost on his agenda. He had a knack for knowing whom he could trust."

"Laney," Evan said, pressing his lips tight. "You're being naive. This is business. Someone stands to gain from The Royals being taken down. This latest

attempt on The Royal San Francisco only goes to show that they're brazen and determined and not afraid of my abilities. That's their biggest mistake. I'll figure it out."

"The manager in San Francisco said the smoke alarm system had short-circuited," Laney said, trying to make sense of all this. Three floors had been involved. Guests were woken in their rooms at 3:00 a.m. when the sprinklers went off. They all had to grab their belongings and get out. Everything got waterlogged. Including the guests. "The complaints on this are the worst we've had."

"There's bound to be lawsuits," he said, his tone laced with quelled frustration. "One man with a weak heart was taken to the hospital complaining of chest pain when he thought the hotel was on fire."

"It's just awful." Laney bit down, her teeth dragging across her lips with worry. "The Royal San Francisco has an impeccable reputation. Yet, everything is made to seem so accidental. It's impossible to believe one person is responsible for all of these problems. Every occurrence so far has happened at a different location."

Evan touched her cheek, the serious glint in his eyes softening when he noted her own genuine concern. She didn't see that look often, but whenever she did, it made her nervous.

"Don't worry," he said, "I'll take care of it."

His hand on her face, the sweet tone he took reminded her too much of the man she'd been with at the Wind Breeze. Evan rarely allowed her to see this side

of him, but when he did she could almost believe he truly cared for her. She let go a troubled sigh and shook her head. "Ultimately, it's my problem, Evan."

"Babe," he said, reaching behind her to pull out the silver barrette holding her hair back. His hands went to her hair, his fingers weaving through, spreading out the tresses. He took his gaze from her hair to look deeply into her eyes. "You have bigger problems."

He kissed her and she responded with a little moan. They'd slept together for the entire week, but after that first morning of lovemaking, Evan hadn't done more than kiss her good-night in the evenings. Every morning she found herself alone in his big bed, wondering why she hadn't felt more than a tiny bit relieved that her husband had left her untouched.

When their lips finally parted, Laney stared into his eyes and questioned him with a whisper, "Bigger problems?"

His lips brushed hers again and he wound his arms around her, meshing his body with hers. Through his slacks, she felt him pulsing with need. Laney trembled and closed her eyes briefly, wanting him with that same sense of urgency. She'd seen his quick glances at her from across the office this week, the way he'd react when she accidentally touched him and the way he'd breathe in her scent when she walked by. He was like a panther, stalking his prey, waiting for the right moment to pounce.

The trouble was that Laney had been equally ready to

pounce. He'd tempted her every night at the penthouse, walking out from his shower, naked but for a towel hugging his waist, dripping water off his thick dark hair, onto his perfectly sculpted shoulders and down his broad chest. She'd seen him shave and dress and do all the things a husband had a right to do in front of his wife. Now that she was feeling more like herself she found the temptation he posed extremely hard to handle.

"You know what I want," he whispered into her ear. "You want it, too. You're healthy, Laney. You're eating well, getting rest. I'm patient. But my patience has limitations."

He ran his hand under her skirt, his fingers caressing her thigh with slick glides, teasing her at the junction of her legs.

"We can't." She thought of all the arguments against this.

"We're going to," he said resolutely. He slid his hand underneath her thong and pressed his fingers to her mound of soft flesh.

"Oh," she moaned, his thrilling touch almost too much to bear.

"I want you, now." He stroked her.

"But we're in the office." She mustered a faint protest, her resistance gone but for fleeting thoughts of being caught by someone walking in.

"And we're in charge."

He stroked her again, his fingers sending exquisite tingles through her body. His other hand cupped her rear

end as his lips covered hers, his tongue stroking over her mouth, until she was wet and ready to melt into him.

"On the desk?" he asked, his breathing labored. "On the floor? The sofa? Tell me, babe."

Her own breaths escalating, she whispered desperately, "Lock the door."

"I locked it ten minutes ago."

Laney was too far gone to care that he'd planned this. It was classic Evan.

"Good thinking." She unfastened his shirt buttons quickly and he helped her with his belt, their hands working like mad to undress each other.

In the back of her mind, she thought about payback. About refusing him this satisfaction. About saying no to him. But she couldn't do it. She couldn't deny them both the pleasure they'd craved this week.

Her husband was too darn hard to resist.

"I'll look on that desk with fondness from now on," Evan said as he peered at her desk, before ushering her out of the office at lunchtime.

"Shh," she said, glancing around the outer offices to make sure no one heard him. She hadn't felt this good in a long time. They'd christened her desk in a crazy rush to find completion and true to his nature, Evan didn't disappoint. Having sex with him had never been the problem. It was every other aspect of their lives that caused her major concern.

And guilt.

Preston's haunting words the other day stuck in her mind, usurping the short-lived happiness she'd found with her new husband.

"Are you forgetting he was the last person to see your father alive? Who knows what he said to aggravate Nolan straight into heart failure?"

Those same questions plagued her every single day. Perhaps, she'd never learn the truth. Perhaps, her marriage to Evan had been the biggest mistake of her life. How could she plan a future with a man she didn't trust?

They rode down the elevator together and once they arrived in the underground parking garage, Laney was ready to head to her own car, when Evan grabbed her hand. "Come with me," he said, his dark eyes gleaming.

He appeared so put-together after their wild encounter on her desk, his hair just right, his tie and suit coat straight when Laney was sure she looked like something the cat dragged in. "Where?"

"I want to show you something."

"I thought you just did."

"Smart-ass." His grin was quick and easy.

"Seems to be your pet name for me, lately."

He ignored her and squeezed her hand. "Come on. Take the rest of the day off."

She glanced at her watch. "I have. But I can't spend it with you. There's just enough time to go home, shower and change."

"For what?" he asked.

Laney hesitated.

Evan stared at her for two seconds before he figured it out. "You have an appointment with the doctor."

She swallowed. "I do. And I don't want to be late."

"You won't be. I'm taking you."

Laney didn't want him with her today. She had doubts that continued to confuse her. She couldn't banish the cold shivers that overtook her body every time she thought that she had betrayed her father by marrying Evan. Whenever he touched her, she felt a moment of panic before desire took over. And now in the aftermath of making love, cold measured remorse set in over her lack of self-control. She turned and started to walk toward her car. "That's not necessary," she shot over her shoulder.

He caught up to her in three long strides and took her arm. She spun around. "Don't bully me, Evan."

"Hey," he said, the sharp angles of his jaw softening when he released her arm. Apparently, he knew he could only push her so far. "I'd like to go with you. It's my baby, too."

Laney frowned. She'd expected a demand. She'd expected his authoritative tone and firm stance. She'd never expected to see this unguarded expression on his face or hear a quiet plea coming from his mouth. Laney thought this might be the closest he'd ever come to asking her permission.

She shrugged. "I suppose you should probably meet the doctor."

* * *

Later that night as they lay in bed, Evan curved his body around hers and set his palm on her belly. "Our son—"

"Or daughter," she added.

"Or daughter," he repeated, and she heard his smile from behind, "is healthy." There was marked relief in his voice.

"I want this baby, Evan. I'm doing my best to stay nourished and well-rested."

He moved her hair aside to kiss the back of her neck. "At one hundred and fifty-eight beats per minute, I'd say the baby is thriving in there."

"It was exciting hearing the heartbeats, wasn't it?" Laney rested her head against Evan's shoulder and sighed.

She'd never thought she'd become a mother so quickly. She'd had those plans set far into her future. Even when she'd been engaged to Justin, they'd agreed to shelve parenthood for several years. But now, seeing that new life inside her from the ultrasound, brought out all of her mothering instincts. The baby bloomed inside her. The doctor confirmed it and aside from her first trimester nausea, all else appeared perfect.

"Mmm." Evan wrapped his arms around her and brought her closer. He'd been in total awe today, too, seeing the clouded image of their child, hearing the heartbeats. He'd asked the doctor questions and stood close to Laney the entire time.

Evan's breath warmed her throat, his hand radiated

heat on her stomach, the strength of his legs encased hers and his erection nudged her from the back.

"Evan?"

"It's okay, Laney. Get some sleep." He moved away from her enough to put space between them, but he kept his hand on her belly.

Tears welled in her eyes.

Sometimes, she really did like her husband.

And if she tried very hard, she might even convince herself she wasn't falling in love with him.

Laney had been at work for three hours the next morning when Evan walked into the office. He'd been dividing his time between Tempest and Royal lately. And after the day they'd shared yesterday, one would think she'd be glad to see him.

Instead of ready to kick his perfect butt out of her office.

"You've gone too far this time!" Laney rose from her chair and came around her desk, her face hot with fury.

Evan stopped. The warm glint in his eyes she'd witnessed when he entered the room vanished. He cast her a cold hard look. "I doubt it, but okay, I'll take the bait. What are you talking about?"

Laney walked past him to close the door then faced him again, her tone a furious whisper. "I'm talking about having Ally investigated! Ally, my father's personal secretary. The woman who's been with Royal for fourteen years! The woman who would take me by the hand for lunch in the cafeteria when my father was too busy. The

woman who let me cry on her shoulder when my mother died and stayed with me for days to console me. The woman who's been like a sister to me here at Royal during these past few months."

"Laney." He shook his head admonishing her for having those feelings, it seemed. "How'd you find out?"

"You left your briefcase on your desk yesterday."

"And you went snooping this morning, right? Still don't trust me?" A tick worked at Evan's jaw. His lips went tight.

"That's not the point. Don't try to throw me off by tossing accusations at me."

"Damn right, it's the point. You don't trust me. Do you or don't you want to save The Royals?"

Laney folded her arms across her middle. "Stupid question."

Evan walked past her to open his briefcase. He pulled out a file folder and lifted it up. "If you saw this, then you know that Ally has some things in her past that don't make her Laney Royal's Personal Saint."

Laney narrowed her eyes. "I didn't read it all." She couldn't. She felt like a slimy intruder, invading Ally's personal life. She'd been more annoyed at Evan, than anything else when she'd found that file.

"She was arrested while in college. For lewd conduct—"

"She was on spring break. For heaven's sake, Evan. The entire sorority minus a few Goody Two-shoes got

hauled into jail. Their parents paid the fines and they were released. She told me all about it."

"She was caught stealing once."

"What? A pack of gum from the grocery store?"

"No, a little more serious than that. This time, it wasn't a sorority stunt. She was alone, caught at an upscale boutique, stuffing clothes into her bag."

"Ally had a rough childhood, Evan. She was raised by a single mother and they barely scraped by. Ally worked her way through college and I know she had good grades. My father gave her a chance fourteen years ago. He was never sorry. She'd become an asset to him."

"Exactly my point. He trusted her. She could use that against him."

Laney hadn't heard of the shoplifting incident, but she still had faith in Ally. Maybe she'd done some things in her youth she was ashamed of, but she wouldn't sabotage the company. She protected Royals like a cautious watchdog. Maybe it was only her husband who managed to abuse trust, like the times she believed him while on the island. "No. I can't believe Ally had anything to do with this."

Evan leaned against his desk, his long legs crossed, his eyes never leaving hers. "Okay. Fair enough. Now, if you can explain away the large deposits made to her bank accounts over the last six months, I'll let it go."

"What?"

"You heard me, Laney. Ally has made three huge

deposits to her account lately. I know what her salary is. Pretty decent, but not enough for her to make those deposits on her own. The problems at the hotel started roughly around the same time as the first deposit. I don't believe in coincidences."

Laney's heart beat with dread. It couldn't be. She closed her eyes. "There must be an explanation for this."

"She's been close to your father for years. She knows things I'd bet that even the vice presidents here don't know."

"I still don't believe it."

Evan pushed away from the desk and grabbed his briefcase. "Babe, if you want to save this company, you have to be willing to believe some things you don't want to."

"But, *Ally?*" Laney bit her lip and sighed.

"Funny, isn't it? You'd rather trust an employee who's hiding secrets, than your own husband."

Laney stared at him. He was right. Every time she thought they were making headway on their marriage, he'd do something that gave her cause to doubt him.

Evan pierced her with a bitter look. "I'd like you to arrange to take a few days off at the end of the week."

"Why would I do that?" Laney asked, shocked at the turn of the conversation.

He headed for the door. "It's time you met my mother."

Nine

"This is the best birthday present I could have imagined," his mother said as she sat next to Laney on the sofa in her retirement home.

Evan had gotten permission from Laney's doctor before he whisked her away to St. Petersburg on a chartered plane for his mother's sixtieth birthday.

Rebecca covered Laney's hand with her own and welcomed her to the family. His mother didn't know how much Laney didn't want any part of him or his family, but he planned on rectifying that as quickly as possible.

"A new daughter-in-law and a grandchild at the same time."

Then his mother shifted her attention from Laney to him. "I'm catching up to my dear friend Larissa

with married children and babies on the way. But you're still in the doghouse for getting married without telling me, Evan."

Evan winced at her admonishment. "I apologized for that, Mom."

"I'm sorry, Mrs. Tyler. It all happened so fast," Laney said, more for his mother's benefit than his. He was sure his wife relished any grief she could bestow upon him. But Laney had a good heart. She didn't want his mother to suffer unnecessarily thinking that he'd deliberately left her out of the wedding ceremony, nonmonumental as it was.

"I'm afraid I gave Evan a bad time of it. And when I finally agreed to marry him, I think," she said, glancing over at him with those pretty blue eyes, "he made the arrangements quickly before—"

"Ah, before you could change your mind?" she asked.

Laney ducked her head slightly, looking a bit embarrassed. "Well, yes. We didn't know each other that well."

"Honey, you knew each well enough to conceive my grandchild."

Laney blinked then, covering her stunned expression well. Evan laughed. His mother had a way of putting things that left her family slack-jawed at times.

"I knew everything I wanted to know about Laney," he said, garnering a flash of immediate anger from his wife. She hadn't spoken much to him since their encounter at the office, only the necessities, but she'd agreed to this trip once he'd told her it was his mother's

sixtieth birthday and he wanted her with him. "We met on Maui for the first time, Mom."

Even though Laney irritated him day in and day out with her doubt and lack of faith in him, Evan still couldn't deny his intense attraction to her. Now, sitting on his mother's rose-patterned sofa as the air conditioner droned in the background tonight, she appeared soft and utterly feminine. Her color had come back and a combination of Florida heat and pregnancy put a healthy sheen on her body. Those blue eyes destroyed him and her womanly form, filling out in places only he would recognize, made him hunger for her every night.

She had ping-ponging emotions for him, one day hot and eager and the next angry and distant. Evan decided taking her on this trip could only help his cause. There was too much tension in the office for them to really work on their marriage.

Months ago if someone told him that he'd be married with a child on the way and planning on "working" on his marriage, he'd have said they were out of their mind. But now, his goal was clear. And he wouldn't let a little thing like his wife's mistrust of him get in the way.

"Yes," Laney said to his mother. "I was vacationing there and, uh—"

Clearly his wife struggled between telling the absolute truth and trying to paint a rosier picture of their union to her new mother-in-law.

"And you hit it off," his mother finished with a quick nod. "I understand. When I met Evan's father, it was

love at first sight. We couldn't stand to be apart from one another. We married in a hurry and never looked back. Oh, I loved him to distraction. We had a good marriage for the short time it lasted. He died rather suddenly. Did Evan share that with you?"

Laney glanced at him. "No, he didn't."

Evan stared at the floor, keeping that part of his life locked up inside. He couldn't look into Laney's eyes. Not now. He didn't want to see the look of pity on her face when she learned the truth.

Then to his relief, his mother patted Laney's hand gently. "It's all right. I'll let Evan tell you himself. When the time is right."

Laney's eyes flashed with curiosity, but she only nodded her understanding. "I'm sure he will."

"Well, you must be tired after your flight," his mother said. "Though you look fit as a fiddle."

Joy and unabashed delight had registered on his mother's face from the moment they'd arrived. Rebecca Tyler was in her element now and thrilled to welcome Laney into her home. Finally, Evan had succeeded in making up for the past. Rebecca would have a grandchild. Evan hadn't anticipated his life taking this turn, but at least his mother would benefit from the marriage and baby on the way. She'd have some well-deserved happiness in her life.

"Evan, why don't you see Laney to your room. Take the guest room just off the hallway. You'll have more privacy there."

Laney rose. "Thank you, Mrs. Tyler."

And his mother stood, as well. "Please, call me Rebecca. Soon, I'll be Nanna."

Laney laughed, the sound foreign to his ears lately. But he recalled the beautiful sound of her laughter on the island, when she wasn't so cautious around him. "I like it. *Nanna,*" she said, testing it aloud.

Evan walked over to his mother. "Thanks, Mom. You get some rest, too. Tomorrow is your big day."

"Ah, turning sixty is no big deal. Becoming a grandmother, now that's something to celebrate!"

Evan kissed his mother on the cheek and was pleased when Laney hugged her, wishing her good-night, as well.

Then he put his hand to Laney's back and escorted her to their room.

Where he planned on seducing his pretty new wife.

Laney leaned against the closed door. "She's a lovely woman."

Evan turned around, his brows lifting. "You sound surprised by that."

Laney closed her eyes briefly. In truth, she was. She didn't know what to expect from Evan's mother. She could have been a hard-nosed shrew, reluctant to give up her son to a woman less than enamored with her oldest child. But she found Rebecca Tyler kind, loving and welcoming. "I am. A little."

Evan shrugged out of his shirt, tossing it aside. His chest exposed, Laney couldn't look away. Evan had a

hard body, sculpted like a bronzed athlete. He walked around the bedroom, unfastening his watch and set it on the bedside table, moving with grace and agility. Laney's breath caught just watching him undress without even a hint of modesty.

He'd always been so comfortable around her, disrobing as if it were the most natural thing in the world for him to do. They'd had sex in a dozen different positions, each time more exhilarating than the next, but now, Laney held on to her inhibitions firmly, a protective cloak shielding her from the dangerous impending storm.

He snapped off the lamp and approached her, wearing only black slacks with the belt unfastened, his skin shimmering in the shadowy moonlight. Laney's mouth went dry like sunbaked sand. "My mother didn't spawn me from the dregs of hell, babe."

"Evan," she breathed out.

He could very well be a devil, so ruggedly handsome with fire in his eyes and a look of raw hunger on his face. If he had his way, they'd both go down in flames tonight. Laney had put him off all week, incensed at his underhanded maneuvers, though she knew he wasn't the kind of man who'd accept her refusals for very long.

"I liked it better when you called me Ty."

"That's not your name," she whispered.

He came closer. "It is, when you say it."

Laney breathed in deeply. "We're in your mother's house, Evan."

He braced both hands on either side of her, trapping her

against the paneled door. "My mother is a sound sleeper. And she's far enough away not to hear your moans."

She gasped quietly. She couldn't deny it. Evan knew all her buttons and he pushed them unmercifully, making her cry out in pleasure every time they made love. "Tell me about your father," she asked out of sheer desperation.

Evan's eyes went wide for an instant. "No."

Laney bolstered her resolve. "I want to know."

"Now's not the time." He kissed her throat and Laney's legs nearly buckled.

She put a hand to his chest. A mistake. His muscles rippled underneath and his skin nearly seared her with heat. It would be so easy to give in to him and take the pleasure he offered. She summoned up every ounce of her willpower. "Please," she said, keeping her hand firm, not quite a shove, but with enough resistance to show him she meant business. "You say you want my trust. Tell me. Share that much of yourself with me."

"You still won't trust me, babe."

"Maybe not. But it'll help me understand you better."

Evan stared at her for a long moment. Something flashed in his eyes, as if he recalled a painful memory. He shook his head then backed up, his face going blank as he kept his gaze fastened to hers.

Laney pleaded with him silently.

Finally, Evan gave a quick nod and she knew he'd taken a great leap of faith. "My mother will tell you my father was a hero. She'd tell you she was proud of him and wouldn't have it any other way."

Evan rubbed the back of his neck slowly. She waited and listened patiently.

He continued in a gritty voice, speaking in the darkened room. "The truth is I'm responsible for my father's death. I took his life, as sure as if I'd put a bullet through his head."

As he explained, Laney's heart bled for the ten-year-old little boy who'd caught the game-winning Rangers' baseball out in the right field pavilion. And who'd been so happy, so oblivious to his surroundings on their way home, that when the ball dropped from his glove and rolled into the street, he'd ignored his father's warning shouts and chased after it. Evan admitted he wouldn't be alive today, if his father hadn't raced into the street to push him aside to safety. John Tyler had been killed on impact, as a truck plowed into him.

"I can still hear that smack, then the screech of brakes and my own horrified screams."

Laney approached him. She took both of his hands in hers. It was awful to think about. She could only imagine the horrible guilt that he held inside. Evan put up walls to keep anyone from knowing him, from getting too close. But right now, she saw only that frightened, guilt-ridden boy. "You can't blame yourself. It wasn't your fault."

"I've heard all the platitudes," he said, his expression cold. "Don't say anything more, Laney. You can't fix this. You wanted to know and I told you."

"Okay, but answer this for me," she said, taking his

hand and placing it on her stomach. "Tell me you wouldn't do the same for your son or daughter? Tell me you wouldn't trade your life for your child's?"

Evan shut his eyes. "My mother's life was never the same. She had to struggle all of her life and raise three boys alone. My brothers suffered, too."

He opened his eyes to witness her understanding nod. "I know that was rough on all of you." Then she covered both hands over his on her belly. "It's what parents do, Evan. They provide for and protect their children. You've made something of yourself and I imagine you've given your mother a good life."

"She's happy." Evan splayed his hand over her belly, rubbing so lightly, his touch the sweetest caress. He lifted his lips only slightly. "Because of the baby."

Laney understood him better now. She understood why he'd been driven his entire life to succeed. She even understood why he blackmailed her into this marriage.

She roped her arms around his neck and reached up to brush her lips over his. "I'm glad you told me," she whispered in his ear.

Evan held on to her a long time, without saying anything. Finally, she looked him deep in the eyes. "Well?"

"I'm glad I told you, too."

Her delighted smile was cut off by the sweeping power of his kiss. She fell into him then, captured by the taste and delicious scents of sweet, addictive desire. Evan picked her up and carried her to the bed, gently lowering her.

She shoved all her misgivings about him aside. She'd accused him countless times of causing her own father's death. What if she'd been wrong? What if she'd only added to his pain and guilt by her accusations? Tender feelings for him rushed in and Laney made a decision to let go of her uncertainties.

Tonight, she would make love to her husband without reservation, fear or doubt.

There would time enough for that.

Tomorrow.

Rebecca's birthday celebration was hardly what Laney would have expected. She sat under a huge beach umbrella on Fort DeSoto Beach, facing the shores of the Gulf of Mexico with her mother-in-law; Rebecca's best friend, Larissa; and her daughter, Serena. Larissa's sons faced off against Evan, Trent and Brock on the sand, playing touch football.

They'd already been on the water, cruising the inlets surrounding the five islands that comprised Fort DeSoto Beach in a boat the Tyler men had rented and subsequently fought to control. Laney met Brock then, Evan's younger brother and had come away realizing that all three men were deliciously handsome, headstrong and competitive.

Brock spiraled a pass her way and Evan raced toward her blanket, kicking up sand. He dived for the overthrown ball and made an incredible catch, landing full force onto his back.

He turned her way and grinned, then rolled over and planted a quick kiss on her mouth. When he bounded up, he called out, "Next time, try throwing the ball *in* bounds, Aikman."

"Hey," Brock said with a playful shrug, "just giving you a chance to impress your wife."

Brock winked at her and was almost hit by the ball Evan tossed at him. Only fast instincts saved him from a smack upside the head.

Laney let go a quick chuckle and felt Rebecca's eyes on her.

"You make my son happy," she said.

Laney silently refuted that statement, immersed in doubt. She'd been blackmailed into this marriage and had never believed Evan really wanted her. He wanted his baby. He was a man bent on control. The child meant more to him than she might have imagined and he'd been persistent in his pursuit.

She witnessed a different side of him today as he bantered with his brothers and the other men. And certainly after the night they'd spent making love, with Evan relinquishing his command in small degrees to let Laney see his vulnerabilities. She felt closer to him than ever before.

Her body still hummed from the way he made love to her last night. He'd lifted her up and set her atop him allowing her to set the pace, his gaze hot, encouraging her as she took all of him in with slow, grinding thrusts until she came with an earth-shattering explosive

climax. And after, they'd spent long moments in each other's arms, both silent, content to let their sated bodies relax against one another.

With Rebecca's expectant eyes still on her, Laney knew she had to respond, but how could she disappoint such a sweet woman? "Our relationship is very complex," she said carefully.

Rebecca patted her hand gently and smiled. "Love always is."

Laney stared at Rebecca, managing a slow unconvincing nod. She wasn't sure she wanted Evan's love or if he was capable of the emotion with anyone besides his family.

Later that evening, they dined at the Dali Museum on Bayboro Harbor, in a private room set up for the occasion. To Rebecca's surprise a dozen other friends joined in the celebration. After dinner, a curator gave them a tour of the surrealist's most famous artwork.

Everyone dressed for the occasion, the Tyler men in tuxedos and the women in gowns. Luckily, Laney thought to pack something elegant, a draping halter with dramatic lines and white lace. She wore two-inch-high sandals that hurt her feet as the night wore on, but she figured she only had a few weeks left of wearing her regular clothes, before she'd have to put together a whole new maternity wardrobe.

Evan's mother seemed to relish every moment of her birthday but Laney noted an added sparkle in her eyes and unmasked pride in her voice when Rebecca introduced

Laney as the newest member of the family. Her emotions torn, Laney couldn't quite believe she was a Tyler now and expected to fit right in, as though the Tylers and the Royals hadn't been formidable competitors.

Evan stayed by Laney's side all evening, sipping Seven-Up to her glass of sparkling mineral water, laughing with family friends, teasing his brothers.

"My mother really loved the gift you gave her," Evan whispered in her ear, once they had a moment alone. He kissed her throat, his lips lingering on the spot just below her earlobe. "Very thoughtful of you."

Laney's pulse sped. She breathed in his musky scent, the hint of cologne that reminded her of tangling in the sheets last night with him. "It's one of my favorite prints. I hoped she would like it."

Months ago while traveling in Europe, Laney had taken a photo of the Eiffel Tower from inside a room on the third floor of an old building, capturing the view through the window's rickety frame. The scene, a study of contrasts from humble to opulent in the French city was backlit by a distant full moon.

She'd been proud of that work and had hoped Rebecca would appreciate her efforts, as well.

"My mother likes art in every form. But she'll treasure that print because it's amazing and because you gave it to her."

Laney smiled and warmth spread through her body. "Thank you."

When Evan's cell phone rang, he frowned and

reached into his pocket. He walked a little bit away, his back to her and all she could hear were mumbled words as he spoke into the phone.

When he returned to her, his frown deepened. "How are you holding up?"

"I'm fine," she answered, a little bit confused. "This is a very nice party, Evan."

He nodded. Then sighed regretfully. "There's been another problem at Royal. We should fly out as early as possible tomorrow morning."

Alarmed, Laney's mind spun at his serious tone. They'd planned on staying the entire weekend and flying home on Monday. Rebecca claimed she didn't see enough of her sons as it was and Laney sympathized. "What kind of problem?"

"Someone broke into your office."

Laney squeezed her eyes shut for a moment and nodded, the betrayal from an employee at Royal headquarters making her heart ache inside. "That means our plan worked."

Ten

The timing sucked.

There was no better way to say it.

Evan had gotten instructions from Code Landon to leak the fact that the entire staff was being investigated in hopes that someone would get nervous and make a mistake. He was certain that one person masterminded the sabotage of the hotels in question. But Evan needed an edge, a clue, something to snare the one responsible. He'd had a hard time getting Laney to agree, but his powers of persuasion finally won out.

So, they'd deliberately spoken too loud around the reception area. They'd dropped the Landon Agency's name several times around the management offices and

Laney had asked pointed, telling questions of the Royal security team.

Evan hadn't expected the trap to work so fast. So instead of spending the rest of the weekend with his family, watching his wife bond with her new relatives and enjoying her company in and out of bed, they had to rush back to Los Angeles.

"Someone's running scared," he said, taking Laney's arm and guiding her toward the Royal headquarters elevator.

Just before the trip, they'd commissioned Landon's best security man to install a new alarm system in their private executive office. No one knew about it but Laney and himself and the head of security, Ralph Blanton.

Evan had already spent thirty minutes questioning the men on duty last night. By the time they'd heard the alarm, whoever had broken in had vanished.

"I have to believe it was someone who knew their way around the offices upstairs," Evan said. "Whoever it was, did their homework. They knew exactly when the security team would be making their rounds, taking their breaks and changing shifts."

Laney nodded, her stoic expression masking her obvious concern. "I've worked alongside these people for years. I know their families, their children."

They stopped at the elevator and looked around. It was Sunday morning and the building was deserted but for the added security Evan had put in place—too little,

too late. "There's only half a dozen or so executives who had the master key to the offices on the penthouse floor."

"And Ally. She's got all the keys. It's still so darn hard to believe," Laney said quietly.

"Because you have a hard time believing the worst in people. Except for me." He scoffed. "Then, you'd believe just about anything incriminating."

Laney pushed the elevator button with force. "My father told me once, 'Always make a good first impression, it might be your last chance.'"

Evan had heard similar words from Nolan Royal the day of their meeting, the day he'd had his heart attack. "Are you saying you didn't have a good impression of me the day we met? Because, babe, I remember it differently." Evan grinned and Laney stared straight ahead at the intricate pattern inside the elevator door.

They rode up to the penthouse and when they stepped out, Laney turned to him. "Okay, I'll admit I found you attractive. You were the distraction I needed to help me forget Justin. We had a hot fling. But that never would have happened if I'd known who you were."

"Are you sure of that?"

Laney paused then nodded her head. "Yes."

Evan believed differently. "One day, I'll tell you what my impression of you was."

"I can only imagine. The lonely, heartbroken girl, just waiting to give up valuable information about the company you planned on raiding, and ripe for a wild ride on the Tyler Express. You sure had me fooled."

He groaned at her choice of words. "The Tyler *Express?* I think not, babe."

She rolled her eyes and shook her head. He took her hand in his and they walked to her office. The door had been closed and locked by the head of security. He'd had to relinquish the code last night, but Evan arranged for a new code to be in place later today.

He walked inside the office first and punched the numbers on the hidden keypad on the wall to turn off the alarm. Laney followed him inside. They scanned the office, searching for anything out of place, checking files and folders in the cabinets. "Apparently, whoever broke in, took off immediately without rifling through any files. Not that they'd find anything. I'm going over all those personal files at my office at Tempest. They're locked away in the safe."

"It creeps me out, just thinking someone broke in here." Laney hugged herself around the middle, looking around the office with a worried expression. "We don't know for sure who it is. It may not be Ally. How can we stop them before they cause any more problems with the hotels?"

Evan came up from behind and wrapped his arms around her, tugging her close. He set her head under his chin breathing in the fresh flowery scent of her shampoo. This wasn't easy on her. Evan wanted to protect her from any more strain, but she'd insisted on being a part of this. He couldn't blame her. The Royals were her hotels and they represented a way to keep her

father's memory and legacy alive. "You can give me a list of everyone with a key, and we'll go from there."

She nodded and turned in his arms. "This is hard for me," she said unnecessarily.

He pressed a soft kiss to her mouth. "I know. But there's one good thing that came from all this—you get to ride on the Tyler Express, any time you want."

Her eyes went wide before she let go a small chuckle.

Evan tucked her head onto his shoulder and held her there for a long while, shielding her, fully surprised by the powerful tug pulling at his heart.

On Monday morning, Preston Malloy entered Laney's office, holding a file in his hand. "Oh," he said as he approached. Evan saw through his futile attempt to hide a frown as Malloy took note of him seated in Nolan Royal's chair. "I'm looking for Elena."

Evan leaned back in his seat eyeing the executive and wondered about his relationship with Laney. He didn't like Malloy and he was certain the reverse was true. But his wife had relied heavily on him right after her father's death and Malloy had come through for her. "She's coming in later today. Is there something I can help you with?"

Malloy shook his head. "I'll wait to speak with her. I've got the reports she requested." He turned to walk out but stopped midway to the door and faced Evan. "You know, I've known Elena since she was a teenager. She's always been levelheaded. Nolan was extremely proud of her accomplishments."

Evan raised his brow. "As he should have been."

"But for the life of me, I can't understand why she married you."

Evan leaned forward, setting a few files in order, then stared into Malloy's eyes, containing his rising anger. "That's what two people usually do when they're expecting a child."

It was worth revealing the truth to see the stunned expression on his face. Malloy sucked in his cheeks and twisted his mouth as though he'd just taken a bite of bitter fruit. "A…child?"

Evan kept his eyes focused on him. "That's what I said."

Malloy came forward to brace his hands on the desk. He leaned in. "Elena wouldn't have gotten that close to a company rival and competitor. She'd known that you were trying to steal the company out from under her father's nose. Unless, of course, she didn't know who you were. If I recall correctly, she'd never met you in person."

"Kind of hard to conceive a child that way."

Realization dawned and Malloy's face reddened. "She *didn't* know who you were, did she? You lied to her and seduced her. You'd stop at nothing to get your hands on this company."

Evan rose from his seat and glared at him.

"No wonder she had a secret wedding ceremony," he said with smug satisfaction. "You must have preyed on her just after her breakup with Overton."

"Malloy, just what's got you so ticked off? That I'm married to Nolan Royal's daughter, or that you aren't the one in the big office running the company?"

Evan's patience had thinned to a sliver. Malloy's accusations rankled his nerves, partly because there was some truth to them and partly because Laney had gotten under his skin. He didn't want Malloy, or anyone for that matter, reminding him of how he'd used her hoping to extract vengeance on Nolan Royal.

"Nolan would roll in his grave if he knew his daughter married you. He didn't trust you. He tossed you out of his office that day and told you to never come back. His first impression of you was dead-on, an unprincipled wildcat and nothing you could've said or done would've changed his mind."

Evan had heard those exact words from Nolan Royal that day, but he'd said them with a smile on his face before showing him to the door. If Royal had believed him guilty of sabotaging the hotels, the man wouldn't have been the least bit gracious. It could have been an act, but Evan didn't think so. Royal relished cutting their meeting short and basically telling Evan he'd rather be struck by lightning than sell his hotels. He'd made his point and the "unprincipled wildcat" statement hadn't been said so much with contempt but with a hint of admiration.

Interesting, how Malloy knew the details of that conversation.

"My wife values your loyalty," Evan began, his voice

steady and controlled, "and your friendship. Don't disappoint her. I owe you no explanations, but I will tell you this. I plan to find out who's trying to undermine this company, so stay out of my way."

Malloy grabbed the file he'd set down.

"Leave it. I'll go over those reports with my wife when she gets in."

Malloy tossed the file onto the desk and walked out.

Five minutes later, as Evan reviewed the financial reports Malloy had left, Laney walked into the office.

Evan's gut reacted. A pure, fresh flowery scent followed her into the room. She wore her long wavy hair down, a black-and-white sundress perfectly fitting her lush curves, flaring slightly at the hips, and bright yellow jewelry around her throat and wrists. Simply put, she took his breath away.

"Hi, beautiful."

She stood just inside the door. "Hi."

They stared into each other's eyes like two silly teenagers gawking at one another.

Laney blinked.

Evan cleared his throat.

His mind wandered far from work and the problems at hand. Lately, whenever she was around, he found himself distracted, thinking about making love to her, caressing her creamy smooth skin, kissing those pouty lips and being buried deep inside her.

Evan felt as if she was finally coming to trust him. But if he told her his latest suspicions, she'd retreat

from him without a doubt. He'd have to keep her in the dark until he was certain of the facts.

"Did you enjoy sleeping late this morning?" he asked.

He'd woken early after a tender night of soft kisses and embraces. Laney had been overly distraught about the break-in and he hadn't pressed her. This morning he'd hoped to remedy that situation by making slow love to her, but she'd been exhausted both emotionally and physically. He'd watched her sleep for long minutes, surprised to find contentment in that. When he'd kissed her goodbye on the forehead she looked up, dewy-eyed and so damn sexy, it was all he could do to keep from pulling her into his arms and stripping her naked.

"Mmm. It was nice, but you should have woken me up."

Evan kept his distance. He had to get to Tempest this morning and Laney posed too big a temptation. "If I had, we'd both have gotten in late today."

Laney mouthed a silent "oh." Then she smiled, her blue eyes gleaming.

"I'm going to Tempest now. But I'll be back at lunch. I want to show you something."

"I think I've seen it." Laney glanced at the desk and her brows rose.

Evan's mind rushed to that day they'd had crazy hot sex on the desk. He walked over to her and lifted her chin with his finger. Then he kissed her. Her lips tasted sweet and her mouth lingered on his making him wish he didn't have pressing business to conduct at his own company. "You have a dirty mind, babe."

Her lips curved up. "You wish."

"I *know,*" he said with a wink. "I'll be back at noon."

Then he left her to do some investigating of his own.

Evan was prompt picking Laney up at noon. Just like the last time, he'd been mysterious about what he wanted to show her. But this time, there were no doctor's appointments or heart-stopping sexual interludes on the desk to interrupt him. He took her hand and whisked her away from the office before she had a chance to discuss any business with him.

That was just not like Evan Tyler.

Business always came first with him.

"Where are you taking me, Evan?" Seated in a brand-new four-door Cadillac Escalade he'd recently purchased as their "family" car, Laney couldn't help but be swept away by his thoughtfulness. She'd made one passing comment about the baby's safety and the fact that his sports car wasn't baby friendly, and last week, he'd gone out and gotten this sturdy SUV.

"Just hang tight, babe. We're almost there."

Evan drove down Sunset heading toward the beach then turned onto a residential street and parked the car in the driveway of a sprawling one-story light blue house with white trim.

"What do you think?

She glanced at the house, then at him. "About what?"

"The house. There's five bedrooms, a study, a huge family room and the backyard already has a playhouse.

It's a princess castle, but if we have a boy, we'll change that into a fort or something."

Laney envisioned a daughter dressed in a frilly pink princess gown in her castle, or a son decked out in buckskin wielding a plastic bowie knife. "You've got it all planned, don't you?"

Evan gave a hopeful nod. "There's an elementary school within walking distance. And the house is half a mile from the beach."

"It's pretty, Evan."

And just what she'd imagined when she was a little girl daydreaming of being married and raising a family.

"If you've already bought it, I'll have to strangle you with my bare hands," she said, without a smile. She meant it. She was tired of Evan making decisions for both of them. If she resigned herself to this marriage, he would have to learn to accept her input on a fifty-fifty basis.

"I promise you, I haven't bought it. But the Realtor's already inside and she's waiting to give us a tour."

"Okay, I'll look at it."

Momentarily, Laney's doubts about Evan fled. He hadn't purchased the house behind her back. That was a start. But to give up her own place and move into a house that they would both share was a gigantic step. It meant stability. It meant solidarity. It meant…forever.

Laney wasn't sure she was ready to do this.

"The house won't go on the market until tomorrow. But it's empty. If you love it, we'll make an offer they can't refuse."

Laney couldn't laugh at Evan's joke. Her heart sped with conflicting emotions. She got out of the car weak-kneed staring at the house. Evan took her hand and they walked side by side up the brick paved driveway. "If you don't see yourself in this house, we'll keep looking," he said.

Some of the tension eased out of her. At least, she had an escape route, if necessary. Though she was sure she'd love the house, she wasn't sure making this move now was the right thing to do. She still had qualms about her marriage.

Amelia Lopez, the Realtor, greeted her with a handshake and a smile. "Wait until you see the kitchen. It's state-of-the-art, but with a homey feel."

And Laney had to agree. She loved the spacious kitchen with a breakfast nook that looked out to a massive backyard. She smiled when she saw the fairy princess castle with a slide that curved down and over a narrow blue foam moat.

The rest of the house flowed, each room being unique and actually…perfect for a new family.

Evan took in all of her comments about the rooms, nodding his head. This was a side to him she rarely saw. He was more approachable, more willing to compromise. "What do you think?" he'd ask, or "You can make whatever changes you think are needed," he'd offer.

When the tour of the house was over the Realtor looked at Evan for an answer. "It's up to my wife," he said. "She has to love it."

Laney appreciated his attitude, but she still couldn't make such an important decision without thinking it through. In that regard, Evan had her beat. He made split-second decisions that were usually right on, when he had to.

"I'm going to need some time to think about it," she said to Mrs. Lopez.

"Of course. The house doesn't go on the market until tomorrow. I expect we'll have a good turnout at the open house, so I wouldn't wait too long to make your decision."

Laney looked at Evan, who'd tried not to show his disappointment. He was a man who always got what he wanted.

"We'll give you our answer," he said to the Realtor as they walked outside, "as soon as my wife makes up her mind. Thanks for the advance showing."

"You're welcome."

They got into his Escalade and Laney took one more glance back before he drove off. "It's really a great house."

"I thought so," Evan said. "But you're not sure about living there...*with me.*"

He hit the nail on the head and she couldn't deny it. She sighed heavily. "It's a lot to take in. I need some time."

He glanced at her, one hand gripping the steering wheel and the other tightly controlled on the gearshift. She noticed him wearing his father's white gold wedding ring on his left hand, a gift he'd received from his mother the other day and she knew what that meant to him.

He draped his hand onto her thigh and stared into her eyes with sincerity. "Take all the time you need."

Laney appreciated his patience. At times, Evan touched her heart in the most surprising ways.

That night, Laney put together a chicken salad and a dish of fresh fruit and they dined quietly on Evan's penthouse balcony. Barefoot, wearing faded jeans and a white tank, looking tanned and vitally healthy, Evan seemed more relaxed than she'd seen him lately.

"You don't have to drink water when we're together. I don't mind if you have a real drink."

He set down his fork and smiled. "Are you trying to corrupt me?"

"Could I?"

"Hell, yeah. In that dress, you wouldn't have to do much."

Laney had seen the appreciative gleam in his eyes this morning when she walked into the office. As his gaze flicked over her much fuller breasts barely contained in the bodice, she had Julia to thank for talking her into buying the Donna Karan sundress. "It's made for you," she'd said. "Wear it in good health, because soon you won't be able to fit into anything without elastic around the middle."

"What would I have to do?" Laney knew she was playing with fire, but tonight she didn't care. Tonight, she felt carefree and a little reckless. Evan had something to do with that. She was drawn to him and the feeling wasn't going away.

Evan shoved his plate aside and pushed back his chair. "Not a helluva lot, babe."

He swooped down and lifted her legs up, planting them onto his lap. The dress rode up her thighs and Evan took note with a low grown of admiration. "First, you'd have to get rid of these shoes."

He took off one sandal. Then the other. "Nice color," he said as he let them drop from his hands.

"They're...uh, canary." Laney had started something and a thrill of excitement coursed through her body.

"Ah," he said, taking one foot in his hand gently and sliding the other hand over her toes. He rubbed his fingers around, making caressing circles.

Laney leaned her head back. "Oh, that feels good."

Then he massaged over her instep, right where the straps of the sandals had dug in all day. Another moan escaped her lips and the dizzying effects of his sensual touch shot straight up her legs to heat the apex of her thighs.

He placed that foot onto his growing arousal, while he worked expertly on the other foot. Laney had trouble concentrating. While he rubbed tension from one foot, the position of her other foot shot rapid fire through her entire body. "Evan."

"What, you don't like my foot massage?" he asked innocently.

The scoundrel.

She bit on her lip and watched as Evan worked his magic on her feet.

"What…else would I have to do?"

"Just sit there and look gorgeous."

He left her feet and leaned forward. Riding his hands up her legs and scooting the chair closer, he reached her inner thighs within seconds.

"You don't waste time."

"Not when I want something."

She didn't have to ask what he wanted. She knew because she craved the same thing.

His fingers found her center and he stroked her just enough to make her crazy, before he stopped and pushed her dress back down. "But I also don't want to get evicted."

He tugged on her wrists and lifted her up, kissing her soundly on the mouth.

She pulled away slightly to whisper, "I thought you owned the building."

He kissed her again, pulling her lower lip out with his teeth. "You *are* trying to corrupt me. I love that." He wrapped his arms around her and kissed her with enough passion to set the whole hotel on fire, backing her up until she was inside the penthouse.

Panting and breathless, she tugged his shirt over his head and exposed his muscled chest. Immediately, she pressed her lips there, kissing him, tonguing his flattened nipples until he groaned aloud.

She was unzipped, out of her dress and on the floor within seconds, the bedroom way too far away for their needs.

Evan unhooked her bra and brought his lips down,

brushing searing wet kisses there. Her hands went into his lush dark hair, splaying her fingers through, holding his head while he teased and tormented her. She arched her body and he took that as a cue to slide his head down, kissing her navel reverently before dipping farther to sheathe her with his hot moist mouth.

He lifted her up, his palms cradling her cheeks and when she arched even higher, he stroked her unmercifully with his tongue. Every nerve ending tingled with electricity. She panted out quick breaths and Evan continued his pursuit, a man bent on being the best at whatever challenge he faced. Now, Laney was glad of it, of him, of his mind-numbing sexual prowess.

She exploded in an orgasm that shattered her completely. She pulsed frantically, trembling with such pleasure that she couldn't contain the moans of ecstasy escaping her throat.

When she opened her eyes, Evan watched her with a light in his eyes she'd never witnessed before.

She knew then, that she was in love with him. Her heart filled with joy at the notion that she loved her baby's father. She wouldn't allow herself to think past that. She'd take the leap of faith needed to trust in him.

Evan rose up to kiss her, his lips tasting of their passion and it was delicious enough to send her body into another upward spiral.

"I need to be inside you," he whispered urgently, parting her thighs with his legs.

She fumbled with his zipper and pushed his jeans down.

"I need that, too," she said breathlessly, ready to take him. He rose up, his arms powerful and bronzed and rippled with muscle, braced on the floor beside her head, his chest close enough to brush frenzied kisses upon.

Her husband, beautiful, stunning, graceful and vital, cast her a hungry look. When he thrust inside her, she closed her eyes and felt the familiar heat and the rightness of it all. She rode the tide of his unnerving passion, lifting, moving under him until neither could hold out another second. Evan thrust deep one last time and she witnessed his amazing climax, the desperate fulfillment on his face as she, too, rose to another peak of pleasure.

When they came down to earth, Evan rolled off her and cradled her into his arms. "I can't imagine a time when we can't do this."

She stroked his jaw, looking deep into his eyes. "You mean when I'm big as a house?"

He nodded. "It'll take all my restraint."

She shook her head. "There are other ways."

Evan's eyes went wide with mischief. "Care to show me?"

She ran a hand through his hair, straightening the strands she'd mussed a few minutes ago. Then smiled down at him. "No. It'll give us something to look forward to."

Evan hugged her tight. "I like the sound of that."

"What?" she asked, her body still pulsing from his expert ministrations.

"You. Me. The future."

Laney smiled deeply and rested her head on his shoulder. She liked the sound of it, too.

That's what worried her the most.

Eleven

The next morning, Laney walked into Preston's office just two doors down from hers. The bronze-plated sign on the door read, Vice President, Finance, but Preston was so much more to her. In many ways, he reminded her of a younger version of her father. Handsome and well-groomed, he had an efficiency about him. He was a problem solver and had been an asset to her father from day one. He always seemed to know exactly how to ease her mind. But since her marriage to Evan, their friendship seemed strained.

She knocked on his door then walked in without waiting for a response. They'd had that kind of relationship with no airs about them, no formality and she wanted so badly to retain that part of their friendship.

"Hi," she said, when he looked up from his desk.

"Good morning, Elena."

She sat facing him, noting his stiff posture. "We haven't had much time to talk lately."

"I've been busy. As usual."

Laney smiled. No one worked harder than Preston Malloy. "I want you to know, I couldn't have taken over my father's position without your help. You've come through for some really rough times in my life and have been such a dear friend."

Preston drew a deep breath. "I've tried to be."

"I haven't had time to speak with you about the break-in the other night."

"No, you don't confide in me like you used to."

His hurt tone caused her injury. "I'm sorry. So much has happened in such a short period of time."

Preston's eyes softened and he rose to sit on the corner of his desk, close to her. He took her hand. "I know. It hasn't been easy on you."

"I don't want sympathy, Preston. I just want to clear the things up. I appreciate your service to the company, but more than that I cherish your friendship. If you're upset about anything, I'd like to know."

He smiled and one dimple popped out. "Elena, how could I not be upset? You married a man who might have killed your father. I know why you did it. You're pregnant."

She gasped. "How did you find out?"

"Your husband was eager to tell me."

Laney slammed her eyes shut. She counted to three,

hoping overriding anger wouldn't destroy the warm feelings she'd had for her husband, but in the end, her patience gave way to building fury. "He had no right to tell you. I wanted to tell you in my own way."

"What would you tell me?" He stood now, looking down at her and she knew he masked his anger with a composed expression. "That you're madly in love with the company's most ruthless rival? That you couldn't live without each other? That press statement he made was bogus. But I figured it out. I know he lied to you when you met him and I know that he blackmailed you into marrying him."

"It wasn't blackmail," she said, defending Evan, God only knew why. She was furious at him for undermining her friendship with Preston. She knew she should have told him the truth right away, but she had trouble admitting how naive and stupid she'd been with her mystery man "Ty." She married him for the baby's sake and because she believed him capable of turning the failing company around. But Preston, of all people, wouldn't have agreed. And his opinion meant the most to her.

"He pressured you. I know his kind, Elena. He lied to you and got you pregnant."

Laney stood to face him, speaking softly, "It wasn't exactly like that, Preston."

"Are you saying he didn't prey on you deliberately?"

Darn if she hadn't thought the very same thing of Evan countless times. "He did, I admit that. And I'm furious that he told you about my pregnancy."

"He enjoyed gloating over it."

"I bet he did." Laney envisioned Evan's self-satisfied face telling Preston that she carried his child. At times, Evan infuriated her and she wondered why in hell she'd conceded to his blackmail.

Maybe her child would be better off without Evan in his life. Maybe she'd given Evan more credit than he deserved. Maybe she shouldn't have let her emotions overtake her good sense.

"It's bad enough to know we're all being investigated, Elena. That sort of thing doesn't lend itself to employee loyalty. Our management VP is threatening to leave Royal. And so many others aren't happy to have their good names questioned. Your father wouldn't have taken these tactics."

Laney closed her eyes. "I know. If I wasn't desperate to save the company and find out who's behind the sabotage, I wouldn't have agreed."

"Personally, I don't believe it's anyone who works for Royal. You and I both know that our competitors have spies. And I hate to say this, but it comes back to your new husband's company. Tempest is one of our biggest rivals. Do you really trust your husband enough to discount that he hasn't been behind this?"

Laney stared at Preston, her mind in a tailspin, her anger at Evan's betrayal muddying her head.

"Answer his question, babe." Evan stood on the threshold of Preston's office, holding the doorknob.

"Apparently, he's not above eavesdropping," Preston said to her.

"Evan, what are you doing here? I'm in a private meeting with Preston."

"Answer his question. Do you trust me?"

Laney stared into Evan's hard, unyielding eyes as he waited for her answer. She hesitated then glanced at Preston, who waited to hear her response. The two stubborn men had put her on the spot. And they'd made this a competition that she'd wanted nothing to do with. There was too much ego and testosterone in the room to suit her. She wouldn't side with either of them, Preston pressing for their friendship and Evan for their marriage.

She'd had it with both of them. "You two can lock horns without me. I'm leaving!"

She strode past Evan, but he took her arm, gently stopping her exit. Holding her in an arm lock, he directed his gaze solely at Preston. "I thought you'd both like to know we've had another hotel *accident*. At The Royal Dallas."

Laney's stomach clenched with the news. She glanced back at Preston, who appeared momentarily stunned.

"In Dallas?" she asked, yanking her arm free.

"That's right. The air-conditioning units are down everywhere in the hotel. You know how hot it is in Texas this time of year. The humidity is enough to smother you. The guests are all demanding refunds and to be placed in other hotels. We're trying to accommodate, but it's a nightmare for the managers."

Laney couldn't believe it. It was as if a vile bug infected one hotel then flew off to attack another and no

one was able to make the catch to squash it. When she glanced back at Preston, his face had paled considerably.

"I'll check into it," Preston offered.

Evan shook his head. "Don't bother. I'm taking care of it. I'm sending a team down to investigate."

"I can handle it," Preston insisted.

"I said no thanks." Evan stood firm.

"You can't possibly trust this guy?" Preston directed the statement to Laney, as if Evan weren't even in the room.

"Preston, be quiet!"

Then she shot daggers at Evan, who tried ineffectually to hide a wide grin, which only infuriated her more. "I'll be in my office. If you know what's good for you, neither one of you will bother me the rest of the day!"

Laney strode out of Preston's office and marched to hers, casting Ally a don't-you-dare-ask look as she passed her desk. She slammed her door and plunked down on her chair, her blood boiling.

Evan left her alone for all of ten minutes before he entered the office. "We need to talk."

Laney had calmed herself enough to stand and tell him off. "You betcha, we do. I'm not through with you, not by a long shot."

Evan closed and locked the door. "Calm down, Laney."

"I'm calm. Calm enough to see the error of my ways."

"Laney," he began slowly in a controlled tone that he reserved for his business rivals. "Run that by me again, and tell me what you're talking about?"

"You had no right telling Preston about my pregnancy, for one! You betrayed my trust. Preston is more than an employee. He's my friend. And you undermined my friendship with him. He's angry and hurt now. This competition between both of you has got to end. For the sake of the company, if nothing else."

"Laney, sit down."

She put her arms around her middle and stubbornly refused with a shake of her head.

"Okay, fine. But I'm warning you. You're not going to like what I have to say."

She shrugged one shoulder. "That's a no-brainer."

"I told him about your pregnancy deliberately."

She rolled her eyes. "Really? I wouldn't have guessed."

He drew oxygen into his lungs then continued on, in that infuriating controlled voice of his. "I wanted to see his expression when I told him."

"He saw yours. You gloated."

"I wanted to rattle him."

Laney shook her head in disbelief. "You did. And you betrayed me at the same time."

Evan approached and Laney didn't like the determined set of his jaw. "I didn't betray you. *He did.*"

"What? How did Preston betray me?"

"If my hunch is correct, he's the one behind the sabotage, Laney. It's been him all along."

"No! Don't you dare even suggest—"

"I'm not suggesting. I've thought it through. It all makes sense to me now. There's no air-conditioning

problem in Dallas. I made it up to see Malloy's reaction. And you know what, he didn't take the news like you did. He wasn't upset or frustrated. He looked *confused*. Confused, because he hadn't ordered that problem in Dallas. It was momentary and he covered his expression after that, but I *saw* it, Laney. I saw, panic and confusion for one instant on his face."

Laney pointed her finger at him. "You're reading into this what you want. You're no body language expert. You don't know Preston like I do."

"Your *friend*, hired all the managers at the hotels in question. He's the only link to all of the problems throughout the country. He covered his tracks, but Landon is damn good at what he does and he sifted through the paperwork to find Preston Malloy at the bottom of the pile when all was finally uncovered. The managers he ultimately hired all had questionable pasts and he must have paid them off to make trouble at their hotels."

"You don't know that, Evan. He supervised the hiring of many upper-ranking employees, but it doesn't mean he knew about any of this. If they had questionable pasts, then they must have gone to great lengths to cover it up."

"You don't want to believe it, Laney."

"I don't. And I won't."

Evan softened his tone. "Babe," he said in his bedroom voice, one that stirred up intimate, sweet memories of their time together. He approached her with a soft look in his eyes. He lifted her chin with his finger and peered deep into her eyes. "I need you to trust me."

She squeezed her eyes shut. He was asking a lot of her. Torn between her strong feelings for him and her desire not to be duped ever again, she didn't know if she could place her faith in him. His actions of late greatly contradicted everything she believed.

She held back tears.

"Malloy said something the other day that got me thinking. When I spoke with your father the day he died, he *had* been smiling, in a smug way and he relished calling me an unprincipled wildcat. Malloy repeated those exact words to me. He knew what your father said to me, *precisely*. He knew, because he'd seen your father *after* my meeting with him. He'd been there, right before your father's heart attack. My guess is that, your father figured it out. He found out that Malloy had sabotaged the company."

Stricken, Laney's heart plummeted. She heard what Evan was saying, but she couldn't process the words. She wouldn't allow herself to believe any of it.

She steeled herself. "You have no proof. No evidence, do you? Why would Preston do something so…criminal?"

"We're working on it. My guess is that he resented your father giving you major control of the company after your wedding imploded. Preston was in line to take over as president. He'd been invaluable to your father. My bet is that one of your competitors made a deal with him to drive The Royals' price way down and with Malloy as their inside man, he'd make sure you'd take the offer."

"But the occurrences at the hotels began happening months before that."

Evan shrugged. "Could be those were real accidents, or Malloy started testing the waters in advance. We don't know who did the initial approach with the idea. Maybe Malloy planned this on his own accord. I've got my investigators working long hours trying to get at the facts."

She bit her lower lip. "You seem so certain."

Evan took her face in his hands and bent to brush a soft kiss to her mouth. "We'll get to the bottom of this."

She peered into his eyes, wanting so much to trust him.

But to believe him, meant to accuse a dear friend and someone she'd trusted her entire adult life of terrible crimes. It meant that Preston Malloy had caused her father's heart attack.

Suddenly, it was too much to deal with. She needed to clear her head. She couldn't think straight with Evan looking deep into her eyes, holding her like a prized doll and making her lips tingle from the searing heat of his expert mouth.

She broke away from him. "I'm going home. To my cottage in Brentwood. Don't come after me. Please."

Evan nodded with a look of concern in his eyes, but he let her go.

She grabbed her purse and dashed out of the office.

Trust him, a voice inside called out.

Have faith in your husband.

Laney wanted to.

With all of her heart.

* * *

As soon as she got home, Laney grabbed her camera and equipment and loaded it all into her car. She drove for miles along Pacific Coast Highway and turned down the narrow two-lane road that led to Point Dume Beach. She'd once been to a wedding here and loved the peace and tranquility of the hideaway little cove.

With the camera slung around her neck, she exited her car and walked along the sandy beach, snapping shots of the landscape, where waves meshed with rocks, where seagulls basked before taking flight, where sunlight streamed onto the water and where a handful of people on colorful beach towels, looked toward the horizon.

Laney found solace here, taking pictures, finding the right angles and light, clearing her mind until the truth beckoned her, seeping right into her soul.

She picked up her cell phone and dialed the office. "Hi, Ally. It's Elena. Do you have time for an early dinner today?"

"I have a ton of reports to get through," Ally said, shuffling papers in the background. "It's the end of the month, remember."

Laney laughed, recalling what a type A personality Ally was. "I remember, but you're always early with those anyway. Besides, I'm officially giving you the rest of the day off. Have a bite to eat with me. There's something I need to talk to you about and it's not work related."

"Really? Girl talk? It's been a while. I'm there."

"Good, I'll pick you up in an hour. And, Ally, don't

make yourself crazy trying to get those reports done before I get there. They can wait."

She heard the smile in Ally's voice. "You know me too well. Okay, I promise."

A while later, Laney sat with Ally in an Italian eatery near the office. They'd ordered antipasto salad and garlic bread and a small white pizza.

"You're not having wine?" Ally asked, as she sipped from her glass of Merlot.

"No, not today. Not for the next six months or so. That's what I wanted to talk to you about. I wanted to tell you, that Evan and I are having a baby. I'm pregnant."

Ally's pretty hazel eyes lit up. "Oh, Elena. That's fabulous! I thought you might be. I mean, the fainting and lack of appetite lately. And honey, don't take this the wrong way, but you did get married in a big hurry."

"It's pretty obvious, isn't it?"

"No, not really. Only to someone who knows you as well as I do."

There was honest joy in her eyes. Laney refused to believe that Ally had anything to do with The Royals' problems.

"Are you happy?" she asked.

"About the baby, yes."

"And your gorgeous hunky husband?"

"He's a different story."

"Do you love him?" she asked, forthright. She and Ally had been through a lot of heartache together and Laney couldn't hold back the truth from her.

"Yes, I've fallen in love with him."

Ally sipped wine and nodded. "You're lucky, Elena. You've got your life planned out with marriage and children."

There was something so painful in Ally's voice that Laney couldn't help but inquire. "What about you, Ally? Is there someone special in your life now?"

Ally nodded and then sipped her wine slowly. Her voice sobered considerably. "Yes, I'm in love, too."

Laney raised her brows. "That's a good thing, right?"

"I'm ashamed to admit, he's married. I didn't know it right away and by the time I found out, I was too much in love to break it off."

"Oh, Ally. I'm sorry."

"It's my own fault for being naive. I just closed my eyes to the truth. But lately, I tell you, I'm thinking it's not worth it. I feel 'kept' and that's not me at all."

"How so?"

"He travels a lot. And he wants me with him when he's gone. So we spend our weekends together and short vacations in the most wonderful places. It's expensive for me. And I've allowed him to deposit money into my bank account for the trips and clothes. Oh, Elena. This is really not the person I am. It's funny what love can make you do."

"I really do understand." Laney consoled Ally, taking her hand in a gesture of friendship, seeing a dear friend, her father's protégée, and a lovely woman who hadn't betrayed the company. It warmed her heart knowing she

hadn't been wrong about Ally. Her only crime had been falling in love with the wrong man.

Right then and there, Laney knew that she was indeed fortunate to have found Evan Tyler. The truth had been right in front of her all along—in the way he treated his family with love. The way he wore his father's wedding ring on his finger with pride. The way he cared for Laney, even when she didn't want to admit his thoughtful gestures were genuine—the baby-safe car, the picture-perfect house, his loving arms around her, always protective and passionate. Laney had come to realize how truly lucky she was to have Evan in her life.

After their insightful dinner, Laney drove Ally to the parking garage at Royal headquarters. "Ally, you've always been a comfort to me. I hope I helped you in some way today."

"You did. I know what kind of future I want for myself now."

"I'm glad. You deserve it."

She hugged Ally tight and watched her get into her car and drive off. Laney was about to do the same when she remembered that she'd left her date book calendar on her desk in the office. Julia insisted on throwing a baby shower for her and Laney promised to call so they could come up with some dates in the coming months.

Laney smiled, thinking that at one time she'd wished she'd never met Evan Tyler in Hawaii. Now, she looked forward to having his baby with an eagerness she could barely contain.

Laney got out of the car and rode the garage elevator up to the lobby, waving to the security guards before taking another elevator to her penthouse office suite. The offices on that floor were empty, the lights out, so Laney entered her office, careful to turn off the new alarm on the keypad. She found her appointment calendar, right where she'd left it earlier today, in her desk drawer.

Grabbing it, she reset the alarm and closed her door, heading back to the elevator. But a mumbled sound startled her and she turned. She heard Preston's voice coming from behind his closed office door.

"The hotels are losing money left and right, but I can't guarantee you they'll sell. Not yet. Yes, damn it. I *know* what you're paying me. I'm telling you I have to keep a low profile from now—"

Laney opened the door.

Preston clicked off his cell phone. "Elena, I didn't know you were here."

Shocked, Laney stared at Preston, her heart beating rapidly. She shook her head, devastated at learning the truth. "Evan was right. It's been you all along. You sold me out to a competitor."

She stepped into his office, facing the man who'd betrayed her father, the man she'd once thought of as a dear friend. "Why, Preston?"

"Why what?" He set his cell phone down, staring at it. "Oh, that conversation? It might have sounded bad if you caught the tail end of it, but I can assure you—"

Laney put up a stopping hand. "Don't! You've lied to me long enough," Laney lashed out, her anger escalating when she thought of the painful, unexpected betrayal. "And my father, Preston. He loved you like a son. He *trusted* you."

"Your father lost his edge a long time ago, Elena. He put you in charge of a company you had no idea how to run when I was the one standing by his side, helping him build his empire, overseeing every little detail, making sure The Royals were top-notch. Always top-notch, Elena. That was me! And what did I get in return for my efforts?"

"You had a great position at Royal, the respect of everyone around you. You had my father's loyalty. And you abused it!"

Preston's eyes flamed with indignation and he spoke with a desperation she'd never before heard from him. "You're delusional, Elena. And you can't prove anything."

He made a move to exit the office. Laney stood in his path, her rising fury refusing to let him get away. "I'm calling the police!"

"Get out of my way!" He shoved her with force and she fell against the wall with a *thud.* Her legs buckled and she collapsed onto the floor, stunned.

Dizzy for a moment, she gazed up to see Evan rushing in with two security guards by his side, blocking the doorway. He took one look at her on the floor, then grabbed Preston by the lapels and pushed him up against the opposite wall. Evan's eyes went black with rage. "You're gonna pay for that."

"Evan, I'm fine," Laney called out, realizing she was dazed but not injured.

Pinning Preston to the wall, he looked back at her. "You sure?"

"I'm sure."

Then Evan gestured for the security guards, who promptly seized Preston's arms. "We have the proof we need to lock you away for a long time. Seems one of your managers ran scared. He confessed to everything, and guess whose sorry name kept coming up?"

He let Preston go, and straightened. "Take him downstairs. The police are on their way."

She watched as Preston was escorted out of his office mumbling words of denial. Then Evan strode over to her quickly and bent to brush her hair from her eyes. "Are you sure you're okay?"

"Y-yes. I'm okay. Heartbroken about Preston."

Evan reached for her hands and lifted her up. He kept his eyes on her, searching her face, making sure she wasn't injured. "He doesn't deserve your concern. He's an out-and-out criminal and we've got all the evidence we need to lock him away. We'll find out who paid him to sabotage the company and they'll go up on charges, too."

Tears rolled down Laney's cheeks.

"Hey, don't cry. The hotels are out of danger now."

"That's not why I'm crying," she said, containing her tears and sniffling as she looked into her husband's handsome face. Laney summoned her nerve. "I'm

crying because I didn't believe in you. I didn't trust you and all the time, you were innocent of my accusations."

Laney realized how much that must have hurt him, when he'd already blamed himself for his own father's death. Evan wasn't responsible for any of it and she'd accused him time and again.

To her surprise and after all they'd been through, he grinned. "Is that all?"

"All? I'd think you'd be furious with me."

"Been there. Done that," he said, taking her into his arms in a protective embrace. "But it's damn hard to be furious with the woman I love."

Laney pulled away to look into his eyes.

Evan smiled. "I love you, Laney. I think it started the minute I saw you sitting at the bar at the Wind Breeze. Remember when I said that I'd tell you what I thought when I first saw you? My first impression was that you were the most beautiful woman I'd ever seen and I wanted you. Before I even figured out who you were. I was completely drawn to you and then after we married, you issued me a challenge. You said I could conquer your body, but I'd never conquer your heart. Big mistake, babe," he said with a shake of his head. "Once I heard that, I knew I'd never be happy until you loved me, because I'd fallen head over heels in love with you."

"Oh, Evan. I love you, too. I have for quite some time, but I couldn't trust you."

"So that means you lied to me, too. You loved me and wouldn't admit it. I guess now, we're even."

Cocky, confident, Evan was back in full form and Laney couldn't love him any more than she did right now. *"Even?"* Laney feigned outrage, when in truth she was bursting with joy. "Sweetheart, it'll take years before we're anywhere close to being even."

"Oh yeah? Is that another challenge?" he asked, playing along.

She reached up to kiss him passionately on the lips, sweeping her tongue inside to stroke him until his breaths became hot and labored.

"Not a challenge," she said, pulling away quickly to stare into his dark eyes. "Just fact."

Evan smiled and gripped her hips, tugging her in until their lower bodies meshed. He whispered in her ear, "I'm taking you back to the Wind Breeze for a real honeymoon. We'll be bold, babe. And I promise you won't get bored."

Thrilled at the thought of going back to the place where they first met, Laney smiled, her heart filled with love. "Sounds wonderful. But first, we have a blue house with white trim and a princess castle in the backyard to buy. I want that house, Evan. I want us to start our life there together."

"Babe, I want that, too. I'll make the call right away." Then Evan gazed at her with a sincere gleam in his eyes. "You're my future now, Laney. You, me and our baby—we'll have a great life."

"We will," Laney agreed, convinced. Finally, she could offer him what he wanted most, her complete

faith and trust because she knew that when Evan Tyler promised something…

…he always delivered.

* * * * *

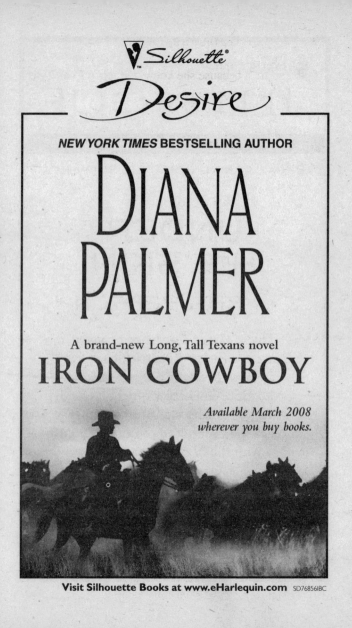

Silhouette®

Romantic
SUSPENSE

Sparked by Danger,
Fueled by Passion.

When Tech Sergeant Jacob "Mako" Stone opens
his door to a mysterious woman without a past,
he knows his time off is over. As threats to Dee's
life bring her and Jacob together, she must set
aside her pride and accept the help of the military
hero with too many secrets of his own.

Out of Uniform
by Catherine Mann

Available February wherever you buy books.

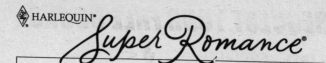

HARLEQUIN®
Super Romance®

Texas Hold 'Em

When it comes to love, the stakes are high

Sixteen years ago, Luke Chisum dated
Becky Parker on a dare…before going
on to break her heart. Now the former
River Bluff daredevil is back, rekindling
desire and tempting Becky to pick up
where they left off. But this time she has
to resist or Luke could discover the secret
she's kept locked away all these years.…

Look for

Texas Bluff

by Linda Warren

#1470

*Available February 2008
wherever you buy books.*

REQUEST YOUR FREE BOOKS!

2 FREE NOVELS
PLUS 2
FREE GIFTS!

Silhouette®

Desire®

Passionate, Powerful, Provocative!

YES! Please send me 2 FREE Silhouette Desire® novels and my 2 FREE gifts. After receiving them, if I don't wish to receive any more books, I can return the shipping statement marked "cancel." If I don't cancel, I will receive 6 brand-new novels every month and be billed just $3.80 per book in the U.S., or $4.47 per book in Canada, plus 25¢ shipping and handling per book and applicable taxes, if any*. That's a savings of almost 15% off the cover price! I understand that accepting the 2 free books and gifts places me under no obligation to buy anything. I can always return a shipment and cancel at any time. Even if I never buy another book from Silhouette, the two free books and gifts are mine to keep forever.

225 SDN EEXJ 326 SDN EEXU

Name	(PLEASE PRINT)

Address	Apt.

City	State/Prov.	Zip/Postal Code

Signature (if under 18, a parent or guardian must sign)

Mail to the **Silhouette Reader Service™**:
IN U.S.A.: P.O. Box 1867, Buffalo, NY 14240-1867
IN CANADA: P.O. Box 609, Fort Erie, Ontario L2A 5X3

Not valid to current Silhouette Desire subscribers.

Want to try two free books from another line?
Call 1-800-873-8635 or visit www.morefreebooks.com.

* Terms and prices subject to change without notice. NY residents add applicable sales tax. Canadian residents will be charged applicable provincial taxes and GST. This offer is limited to one order per household. All orders subject to approval. Credit or debit balances in a customer's account(s) may be offset by any other outstanding balance owed by or to the customer. Please allow 4 to 6 weeks for delivery.

Your Privacy: Silhouette is committed to protecting your privacy. Our Privacy Policy is available online at www.eHarlequin.com or upon request from the Reader Service. From time to time we make our lists of customers available to reputable firms who may have a product or service of interest to you. If you would prefer we not share your name and address, please check here. ☐

SDES07

$1.00 OFF

The bestselling Lakeshore Chronicles continue with *Snowfall at Willow Lake*, a story of what comes after a woman survives an unspeakable horror and finds her way home, to healing and redemption and a new chance at happiness.

SUSAN WIGGS

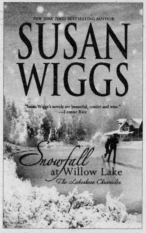

NEW YORK TIMES BESTSELLING AUTHOR

SUSAN WIGGS

"Susan Wiggs's novels are beautiful, tender and wise."
—Luanne Rice

Snowfall at Willow Lake
The Lakeshore Chronicles

On sale February 2008!

SAVE $1.00 off the purchase price of **SNOWFALL AT WILLOW LAKE** by Susan Wiggs.

Offer valid from February 1, 2008, to April 30, 2008.
Redeemable at participating retail outlets. Limit one coupon per purchase.

5 2 6 0 8 1 6 8

5 65373 00076 2 (8100) 0 11463

MSW2493CPN

Silhouette

Desire

COMING NEXT MONTH

#1849 PRIDE & A PREGNANCY SECRET—
Tessa Radley
Diamonds Down Under
She wants to be more than his secret mistress, especially now
that she's pregnant with his heir. But she isn't the only one with a
secret that could shatter a legacy.

#1850 TAMING CLINT WESTMORELAND—
Brenda Jackson
They thought their fake marriage was over...until they discovered
they were still legally bound—with their attraction as strong as ever.

#1851 THE WEALTHY FRENCHMAN'S PROPOSITION—
Katherine Garbera
Sons of Privilege
Sleeping with her billionaire boss was not on her agenda. But
discovering they were suddenly engaged was an even bigger
surprise!

#1852 DANTE'S BLACKMAILED BRIDE—Day Leclaire
The Dante Legacy
He had to have her. And once he discovered her secret, he had the
perfect opportunity to blackmail his business rival's daughter into
becoming his bride.

#1853 BEAUTY AND THE BILLIONAIRE—
Barbara Dunlop
A business mogul must help his newest employee transform from
plain Jane to Cinderella princess...but can he keep his hands off
her once his job's done?

#1854 TYCOON'S VALENTINE VENDETTA—
Yvonne Lindsay
Rekindling a forbidden romance with the daughter of his sworn
enemy was the perfect way to get his revenge. Then he discovers
she's pregnant with his child!

Dear Reader,

I love visiting Hawaii and I love chance encounters. The idea of a corporate raider accidentally meeting up with his rival's beautiful daughter and hatching a scheme to take revenge on his competitor was a story I *had* to write. Put them all together, an exotic location, red-hot chemistry from the get-go, a hunky millionaire and a hotel heiress, add a little deception and intrigue along the way, and you have *The Corporate Raider's Revenge*.

But sexy Tempest Hotel owner Evan Tyler doesn't know what he's gotten himself into when Elena Royal turns the tables on him. Elena isn't a pushover, and I enjoyed every moment writing the battle of wills between the two.

I hope you enjoyed meeting the Tylers. There'll be more stories coming soon with Evan's brothers—those hard-driving, heart-stopping Tyler heroes.

Happy reading!

Charlene Sands

REAL MEN STILL EXIST…on the pages of a
Charlene Sands romance. Visit www.charlenesands.com.

Damn, She Was A Beauty.

Then Evan realized who she was. Elena Royal.

His rival in the hotel business, Nolan Royal, had only the one child, and she usually kept a low profile. Evan almost could give Nolan Royal credit for keeping the media out of his daughter's life.

Almost.

But because Nolan Royal had been a *royal* pain lately, cheating Evan out of a hotel buyout that he'd been working on for two years, he couldn't even give the man his due for protecting his daughter. Evan still burned from Royal's deliberate and dishonorable tactics.

He meant to make Royal pay.

Evan turned to Elena, "Want to get un-bored?"

She raised her eyebrows and he could tell she was intrigued. "What do you have in mind?"